THE OLD ENGLI:

CLARA REEVE (1729–1807) was born in Ipswich, the eldest daughter among the eight children of William Reeve, an Anglican minister, and Hannah Smithies Reeve, daughter of the jeweller and goldsmith to King George I. She was initially educated at home, and claimed later in her life that her childhood reading included parliamentary debates as well as histories of Britain, Greece, and Rome. Following the death of her father in 1755, Reeve moved from Ipswich to Colchester, along with her mother and two of her sisters. Here she eventually acquired her own lodgings, and went on to live a relatively isolated but nonetheless active life. Reeve appears to have started writing at a young age, but did not publish any of her work until the collection of verse *Original Poems on Several Occasions* (1769); this was followed in 1772 by a translation of John Barclay's Latin romance *Argenis*. After the success of *The Old English Baron* (1778), a revised edition of *The Champion of Virtue*, Reeve went on to write a number of works of fiction, including novels of contemporary life such as *The Two Mentors* (1783) and *The School for Widows* (1791), and the historical romance *Memoirs of Sir Roger de Clarendon* (1793). Reeve wrote widely in different genres, and her other works include the conduct book *Plans of Education* (1792), and the children's history *Edwin, King of Northumberland* (1802). Aside from *The Old English Baron*, Reeve is best known for her ambitious and innovative work of literary history *The Progress of Romance* (1785). Reeve died in Ipswich in 1807.

JAMES TRAINER edited *The Old English Baron* for the Oxford English Novels series in 1967, and has recently retired from the German Department at the University of Stirling.

JAMES WATT is Lecturer in the Department of English and Related Literature at the University of York. He is the author of *Contesting the Gothic: Fiction, Genre, and Cultural Conflict* (1999), and essays on Romantic Orientalism.

OXFORD WORLD'S CLASSICS

For over 100 years Oxford World's Classics have brought readers closer to the world's great literature. Now with over 700 titles—from the 4,000-year-old myths of Mesopotamia to the twentieth century's greatest novels—the series makes available lesser-known as well as celebrated writing.

The pocket-sized hardbacks of the early years contained introductions by Virginia Woolf, T. S. Eliot, Graham Greene, and other literary figures which enriched the experience of reading. Today the series is recognized for its fine scholarship and reliability in texts that span world literature, drama and poetry, religion, philosophy and politics. Each edition includes perceptive commentary and essential background information to meet the changing needs of readers.

OXFORD WORLD'S CLASSICS

CLARA REEVE

The Old English Baron

Edited by
JAMES TRAINER
With an Introduction and Notes by
JAMES WATT

OXFORD
UNIVERSITY PRESS

OXFORD

UNIVERSITY PRESS

Great Clarendon Street, Oxford OX2 6DP

Oxford University Press is a department of the University of Oxford.
It furthers the University's objective of excellence in research, scholarship,
and education by publishing worldwide in

Oxford New York

Auckland Bangkok Buenos Aires Cape Town Chennai
Dar es Salaam Delhi Hong Kong Istanbul Karachi Kolkata
Kuala Lumpur Madrid Melbourne Mexico City Mumbai Nairobi
São Paulo Shanghai Taipei Tokyo Toronto

Oxford is a registered trade mark of Oxford University Press
in the UK and in certain other countries

Published in the United States
by Oxford University Press Inc., New York

Editorial material © James Watt 2003

The moral rights of the author have been asserted
Database right Oxford University Press (maker)

First published as an Oxford World's Classics paperback 2003
Reissued 2008

British Library Cataloguing in Publication Data

Data available

Library of Congress Cataloging in Publication Data

Data available

ISBN 978-0-19-954974-0

13

Typeset in Ehrhardt
by RefineCatch Limited, Bungay, Suffolk
Printed and bound in Great Britain
by Clays Ltd, Elcograf S.p.A.

CONTENTS

INTRODUCTION

In a letter to William Cole in August 1778, Horace Walpole
witheringly dismissed *The Old English Baron* as a work so
'stripped of the marvellous . . ., except in one awkward attempt at
a ghost or two, that it is the most insipid dull thing you ever saw';
'what makes one doze', he added, 'seldom makes one merry'.[1]
Almost fifty years later, Sir Walter Scott gave a similar verdict in
the brief memoir of Reeve that he contributed to the Novelist's
Library edition of her work. Although he noted its 'competent
command of those qualities which constitute a good romance',
Scott described *The Old English Baron* as 'tame and tedious, not
to say mean and tiresome', and represented Reeve as a secluded
'authoress', whose 'acquaintance of events and characters derived
from books alone'.[2] A number of readers since Scott have been
almost as disparaging, and *The Old English Baron* is still liable to
be found wanting when judged against a normative standard of
'Gothic' narrative effects or thematic concerns. Reeve's critical
reputation has grown significantly in the last few decades,
nonetheless, not least because of the increasingly detailed and
sophisticated attention that has been paid to the diverse varieties
of eighteenth-century women's writing. What Walpole and Scott
presented as Reeve's creative inhibition is more likely to be
understood today, therefore, as a function of her larger critical
and moral project; once marginalized as a literary-historical
curiosity, *The Old English Baron* now appears instead as a
boldly revisionist work, providing an important and influential
contribution to the development of Gothic fiction.

Reeve's efforts to establish herself as an independent writer

---

[1] Horace Walpole, letter to William Cole, 22 Aug. 1778, *The Yale Edition of the
Correspondence of Horace Walpole*, ed. W. S. Lewis (New Haven: Yale University Press,
1937–83), xl. 379.

[2] Sir Walter Scott, 'Prefatory Memoir to Clara Reeve', *The Novels of Sterne, Gold
smith, Dr Johnson, Mackenzie, Horace Walpole and Clara Reeve. To which are prefixed,
Memoirs of the Lives of the Authors*, Novelist's Library (Edinburgh, 1823), pp. lxxxi,
lxxxv, lxxxvi.

began relatively late in her life with a collection of miscellaneous short works published in 1769, under the initials 'C.R.', entitled *Original Poems on Several Occasions*. In its preface, as well as in some of the collected poems, Reeve intermittently alluded to her personal experience of the prejudices of 'mankind in general' against female authorship. Reeve also claimed that the recent successes of other women had encouraged her to compete 'for the same advantages',[3] however, and she subsequently became a prolific writer, albeit in apparent isolation from any larger network of learning and sociability. Shortly after *Original Poems*, Reeve published *The Phoenix* (1772), a translation of John Barclay's prose romance *Argenis*, which had first appeared in Latin in 1621. Though presented anonymously, *The Phoenix* was nonetheless an ambitious project by which Reeve laid claim to the kind of status enjoyed by prominent learned women such as Elizabeth Carter, translator of *All the Works of Epictetus* in 1758. Reeve's first work of fiction *The Champion of Virtue*, published in 1777, displayed a similar kind of cautious assertiveness. Reeve again remained anonymous, identifying herself as 'the Editor of the Phoenix' on the title page, but her description of the work as 'A Gothic Story' daringly affiliated it—to Walpole's obvious annoyance—with *The Castle of Otranto* (1764–5). In the preface to the revised second edition of her novel, published in 1778 as *The Old English Baron*, Reeve emphasized the 'extreme reluctance' (p. 4) with which she declared her authorship, but at the same time openly declared her work to be 'the literary offspring of the Castle of Otranto' (p. 2).

Reeve versus Walpole

Reeve stated in her preface that *The Old English Baron* was 'written upon the same plan' (p. 2) as *Otranto*, and it is clearly a derivative work in many ways. Following the example of Walpole, albeit in much less detail, Reeve initially presented herself, in *The Champion of Virtue*'s 'Address to the Reader', as an editor who had 'translated' a manuscript 'in the old English language'

---

[3] Clara Reeve, *Original Poems on Several Occasions* (London, 1769), p. xi.

for a modern audience (see Appendix 1). Like Walpole, too, Reeve built the plot of her work around the discovery and reversal of an act of usurpation, set in train by the return to England of the 'worthy Knight' (p. 5) Sir Philip Harclay. Sir Philip finds that his childhood friend Arthur, Lord Lovel is no longer alive, and that the castle and estate of the family are now in the hands of Baron Fitz-Owen, who had bought them from his brother-in-law, also the kinsman of the dead man, Sir Walter Lovel. The villainous Sir Walter Lovel is not developed to the same extent as Walpole's Manfred, since he is offstage for most of the work, but the figure of the dispossessed heir Edmund Twyford—encountered by Sir Philip on his first visit to the castle—is clearly modelled on Theodore, the virtuous peasant eventually revealed to be the true Prince of Otranto. As in *Otranto*, the final resolution of *The Old English Baron* is brought about with the aid of supernatural agency. During his trial of courage in the apartment in which his father had been murdered, Edmund is visited in a dream by his parents ('a Warrior, leading a Lady by the hand'), who declare him to be the 'sweet hope of a house that is thought past hope!' (p. 38). This recognition of Edmund's true status is emphatically endorsed when he later returns to Lovel Castle as its rightful owner, and 'every door in the house' (p. 115) spontaneously flies open to receive him.

The obvious similarities between *Otranto* and *The Old English Baron* accentuate the predictability of the latter's plot; as Anna Laetitia Barbauld observed in her 1810 introduction to Reeve's work, 'we foresee the conclusion before we have reached twenty pages'.[4] Far from being straightforwardly imitative, however, *The Old English Baron* also rewrites Walpole's example. In the second preface to *The Castle of Otranto*, Walpole had expressed his desire to restore fancy and imagination to the modern novel, in order to shake off its constraining 'adherence to common life'.[5] While endorsing Walpole's stated aim, Reeve claimed in her preface that *Otranto* overdid its use of supernatural effects, and employed

[4] Anna Laetitia Barbauld, *The British Novelists* (London, 1810), vol. xxii, p. ii.

[5] Horace Walpole, *The Castle of Otranto*, ed. W. S. Lewis and E. J. Clery (Oxford: Oxford University Press, 1998), 9.

them in such an extravagant way as to exceed the 'limits of credibility' (p. 3), and dissolve the enchantment that it seemed to
promise. Like many late-eighteenth-century readers, Reeve
characterized *Otranto* as a work that was more ridiculous than
sublime, and read its bizarre excess as a product of Walpole's
'aristocratic' appetite for diversion and display. Walpole in turn
was hostile towards what he saw as Reeve's presumptuous imita-
tion of *Otranto*, claiming that *The Old English Baron* showed such
little imagination 'that any trial for murder at the Old Bailey
would make a more interesting story'.[6] Reeve's preface openly
avowed the relative restraint and sobriety of her work, nonetheless, in the context of a larger revisionist project. Alluding to the
distinction between nature and poetry drawn by Sir Philip
Sidney, Reeve contrasted the functions of history and romance:
'History represents human nature as it is in real life', she claimed,
whereas 'Romance' displays 'the amiable side of the picture' and
may therefore be 'rendered subservient to good and useful purposes' (p. 2). While some of her contemporaries debated the
nature of sublime experience, or the conjunction of terror and
pleasure, Reeve was wary about the prioritization of affect as an
end in itself. The proper 'business of romance' (p. 3), according
to Reeve, was first to gain the reader's attention, as Walpole had
done, but then to channel or direct it to a socially desirable end,
following the practice of a writer such as Samuel Richardson.
(One of Richardson's daughters, Martha Bridgen, played an
important role during the revision of *The Champion of Virtue* into
The Old English Baron.) Reeve's pioneering critical survey, *The
Progress of Romance* (1785), outlined her interest in the formative
impact of imaginative writing at much greater length, and contributed towards a larger reappraisal of the genealogy of romance
and the canon of prose fiction. In a series of dialogues, the authorial surrogate Euphrasia confronts the initial mockery of her male
friend Hortensius, and in the process establishes her credentials
as a learned woman, and an independent and knowledgeable
critic. Taking on one of the most renowned writers in the

[6] Horace Walpole, letter to William Mason, 8 Apr. 1778, *Correspondence*, xxviii.
381–2.

country, the short preface quoted above must itself also be seen as a part of Reeve's bid to construct for herself an authoritative and morally exemplary critical position, and thereby legitimize her revision of Walpole's work.[7]

The Old English Baron engages with *The Castle of Otranto* on many levels, but perhaps the most tangible way in which Reeve's work revises Walpole's is by employing supernatural effects in a more sparing and strategic fashion. The comic villains Markham and Wenlock seem to follow Walpole's bungling domestics Diego and Jaquez in their response to the armour-clad ghost of Lord Lovel in the castle's haunted apartment, visually depicted in the frontispiece to the 1780 edition of the novel. As well as providing a comic interlude, though, the trembling reactions of Markham and Wenlock serve to reflect their guilt at being involved in the plot against Edmund; unable to 'sleep in quiet in his own room' (pp. 44–5), Sir Walter Lovel is similarly shown to betray a guilty conscience in his earlier decision to leave and then sell the castle. Characters such as Edmund, along with Father Oswald and the family servant Joseph, by contrast, respond to the mysteries of the apartment in a calmer and more deliberate manner. Reeve's work employs a range of formulaic effects to evoke Edmund's surroundings during his earlier trial of courage in the same rooms (an episode later pastiched by Scott in *The Antiquary* (1816)): 'The furniture, by long neglect, was decayed and drooping to pieces; the bed was devoured by the moths, and occupied by the rats.' Edmund's lamp is blown out by the wind to leave him in 'utter darkness', and he hears a 'hollow rustling noise like that of a person coming through a narrow passage', at which point 'all the concurrent circumstances of his situation struck upon his heart, and gave him a new and disagreeable sensation' (p. 36). Almost immediately, however, Edmund's fear is overridden by his Christian faith. The episode serves even to strengthen his resolve: 'What should I fear? I have not wilfully offended God, or man; why, then, should I doubt protection?' Reeve's hero regains his confidence in the power of prayer, and resigns himself to 'the will

---

[7] See Laura Runge, *Gender and Language in British Literary Criticism, 1760–1790* (Cambridge: Cambridge University Press, 1997), 155–63.

of Heaven' (p. 36), before signalling his desire to speak to the
spirit (in keeping with Reeve's minimal evocation of the supernatural, Edmund in fact subsequently encounters Joseph rather
than a ghost). The following night, Edmund, Joseph, and Oswald
investigate the violent noises they hear, and their discovery of the
portraits of Lord and Lady Lovel, along with a bloodstained suit
of armour, helps them to start piecing together the truth about
Edmund's status, and the fate of his parents. By the time of their
final night in the haunted rooms, Edmund and his companions
are inured to manifestations of the supernatural: they hear 'the
same groans as the night before in the lower apartment', but
'being somewhat familiarized to it, they were not so strongly
affected' (p. 60).

Occasional moments of bathos like this are perhaps remin-
iscent of Walpole's work (echoing, for example, the description of
Manfred being 'almost hardened to preternatural appearances'
on the falling of the gigantic sword in *Otranto*[8]). *The Old English
Baron* has little if any of *Otranto*'s tonal ambiguity, however, and
its scheme of punishment and reward, like its representation of
the supernatural, is much more straightforward. Whereas Walpole's Manfred complains about paying the price for the deeds of
his grandfather, Sir Walter Lovel is shown to be directly respon-
sible for orchestrating the murder of his kinsman Arthur; unlike
Manfred, in addition, he has no family to suffer the consequences
of his actions. After his defeat by Sir Philip Harclay in the trial by
combat, Sir Walter Lovel confesses not only his culpability but
also his motivation, admitting that the 'baleful passion of envy'
(p. 91) was at the root of his crimes. The guilty man draws the
requisite moral from his own story, moreover, stating that 'nothing can be concealed from the eye of Heaven' (p. 92)—a point
forced home by the novel's refrain about 'the over-ruling hand
of Providence, and the certainty of RETRIBUTION' (p. 136). If
'retribution' is said to be inevitable, though, Reeve's work
depicts no clamour for revenge. Sir Walter Lovel remains
haughty and reserved, and reluctant to surrender his estates, but

[8] Walpole, *Otranto*, 66.

he is nonetheless presented as a redeemable figure; after a failed escape attempt, he is banished to 'the Holy Land' (p. 119) in the company of Sir Philip Harclay's attendant Zadisky, and given the chance to begin a new life in the service of the Greek emperor. Initially treated as an outcast, Sir Walter Lovel is eventually rewarded with a post in the Greek army, and marries the daughter of a fellow officer. Reeve offers no direct commentary on his rehabilitation, but it is significant that her villain ends the work engaged in the enterprise in which Sir Philip Harclay had earned such distinction—defending the frontiers of the Byzantine Empire against the encroachments of the Ottoman Turks.

Bourgeois Revisionism?

In his introduction to the Oxford English Novels edition, James Trainer stated that Reeve's work reads like 'a sermon based on an Old Testament text'—'freshly and fluently delivered, without great pretension in thought or ethics, but full of optimism and cheer for the man whose conscience is clear'.[9] In contrast to *Otranto*, *The Old English Baron* concludes on a celebratory note, with the formal burial of Lord and Lady Lovel rapidly followed by Edmund's marriage to Lady Emma Fitz-Owen. If Reeve's work ties all the loose ends of its plot, however, the section that precedes this festive conclusion has proved more difficult for critics and readers to assimilate, and all the more obtrusive, perhaps, given the generally condensed and sparse nature of Reeve's narrative. After Sir Walter Lovel's guilt and Edmund Lovel's status are confirmed, about two-thirds of the way through the work, the problem remains of how the rival claims on the lands of the family are to be adjudicated. Sir Philip Harclay advances the cause of the rightful heir Edmund, stating that he deserves compensation for the length of time that he had 'unjustly been kept out' (p. 108) of his estate; fearing that he stands to be dispossessed, meanwhile, Sir Robert Fitz-Owen presses the case of his father, who had in good faith paid cash for

[9] Clara Reeve, *The Old English Baron*, ed. James Trainer (Oxford: Oxford University Press, 1967), pp. xi–xii.

the castle. The filial affection between the Baron Fitz-Owen and Edmund, cemented by the latter's marriage to the Baron's daughter, eventually overrides the tension that is generated by these competing property claims—Sir Robert Fitz-Owen is given possession of the estate that belonged to the banished Sir Walter Lovel, while his father decides to retire to his castle in Wales. Reeve's protracted emphasis on the precise detail of the final property settlement, and its legal confirmation, has nonetheless seemed to many readers to be problematically discontinuous with the rest of the work. As the critic John Dunlop complained, for example, the 'incidents . . . of real life' are 'sometimes too accurately represented' in *The Old English Baron*, resulting in a disjunction between 'the gigantic and awful features of the romance' and the anxieties of 'heroic and important characters' about 'settlements, [the] stocking of farms, and household furniture'.[10] In a similar vein, Scott drew attention to the surfeit of 'prolix, . . . and unnecessary details' in Reeve's work, exemplified most prominently by 'the grave and minute accounting' of Sir Philip Harclay and Baron Fitz-Owen.[11]

Like Dunlop and Scott, many readers have claimed not only that *The Old English Baron* lacks invention, but also that its circumstantial detail seems to be out of keeping with its romance framework. Such flaws have often been read as defects of skill or craft, consequent upon a certain gaucheness or inexperience on Reeve's part; 'nowhere else' in the Gothic, as J. M. S. Tompkins has observed, 'do we find knights regaling on eggs and bacon and suffering from the toothache'.[12] The 'minute accounting' identified by Scott might also be read, however, as a symptom of the kind of romance revisionism that Reeve was undertaking. While *The Old English Baron* clearly presents itself as a work ruled by moral imperatives, seeking to tone down the excesses of *Otranto*, several recent critics have claimed further that Reeve's rewriting

---

[10] John Dunlop, *The History of Fiction: being a Critical Account of the most celebrated Prose Works of Fiction, from the earliest Greek Romances to the Novels of the Present Age*, 3 vols. (London, 1814), iii. 384.

[11] Scott, 'Prefatory Memoir', p. lxxxvi.

[12] J. M. S. Tompkins, *The Popular Novel in England, 1770–1800* (London: Constable & Co., 1932), 229–30.

of Walpole can be seen to stage the ascendancy of a distinctly 'bourgeois' set of values. The last third of *The Old English Baron* depicts at some length the disposal and distribution of property among characters who seem to belong, as is often noted, more to the middle classes of the eighteenth century than the aristocracy of the fifteenth century. Most importantly, Reeve's work does not just recognize the legitimate nobility of its hero, in the manner of Walpole's *Otranto*, but also presents him as the embodiment—in Gary Kelly's terms—of late-eighteenth-century professional middle-class virtues.[13]

Whichever character it refers to, 'The Champion of Virtue' might seem to be a more appropriate title than 'The Old English Baron' for Reeve's work, because of the way that it foregrounds the thematic centrality of the hero's merit. At the outset, while he is still thought to be the son of a labourer, the 'merit' (p. 14), the 'good qualities', and the 'extraordinary genius and disposition' (p. 14) of Edmund Twyford are repeatedly emphasized. Despite being possessed of 'that inward consciousness that always attends superiour qualities', Edmund is mindful of his 'low birth and dependant station', and checks 'the flames of ambition' (p. 21) (Sir Robert Fitz-Owen seeks to remind him of his lowly status with the injunction that he should 'know himself' p. 22). Believing that he is of humble origin, Edmund allows his conduct to speak for itself, fashioning himself as a transparently readable figure, with 'nothing but my character to depend on' (p. 30); as he says to the family servant Joseph at an early stage, 'words are all my inheritance' (p. 21). Edmund's shining qualities excite the envy of some of those around him, notably Sir Robert and his cabal, just as his father's 'merit' and 'graces and person of mind' (p. 91) had rankled with the man who orchestrated his murder. These qualities also make Edmund an object of admiration and affection, though, and a deserving object of patronage for his twin guardians, Baron Fitz-Owen and

---

[13] Gary Kelly, 'Introduction: Clara Reeve', in id. (ed.), *Bluestocking Feminism: Writings of the Bluestocking Circle, 1738–1785* (London: Pickering & Chatto, 1999), vi: *Sarah Scott and Clara Reeve*, p. xxxii. See also Kelly, *Women, Writing, and Revolution, 1790–1827* (Oxford: Clarendon Press, 1993), 187–8.

Sir Philip Harclay, who declare their support for 'merit in distress' (p. 18).

Edmund is first introduced to the reader as the victor in an archery contest, and his military exploits in France are deemed worthy of a knighthood; after Sir Robert Fitz-Owen has pledged to contend with him for glory, Edmund heads an ambush against a French convoy and kills its leader. Even if he sometimes trumps members of the aristo-military caste at their own game, however, Edmund's military prowess is only briefly represented, and he is shown instead to be possessed of a modern, eighteenth-century sensibility. While he remains an active and worldly figure in comparison with a character such as Henry Mackenzie's Harley, in *The Man of Feeling* (1771), Edmund performs a refined or softened version of masculinity, as exemplified by the fact that his eventual marriage is said to offer a model of 'conjugal affection and happiness' (p. 134). Throughout the work, Reeve's hero bonds or connects with others in an expressive, sentimental fashion, in such a way as to temper differences of rank. Before his true status is recognized, Edmund declares a desire 'to live and die' in the service of Baron Fitz-Owen; for the Baron, Edmund's character 'engages the heart' (p. 17) to such an extent that he is unable to part with him. Edmund is similarly devoted to 'his beloved Master William', the Baron's youngest son, who in turn 'treated him in public as his principal domestic, but in private as his chosen friend and brother' (p. 22). Reeve's work describes numerous such affective or familial relationships, and Edmund constantly seeks the approval of characters who in turn compete for his regard. Edmund is 'patient and enduring when his class position requires it', as Ruth Perry has argued, and 'supplicating rather than demanding, grateful rather than triumphant, when he receives undeniable proof of his real social position'.[14] The fact that Reeve's hero is eventually proved to be of noble birth finally circumvents any tension between merit and rank (along with any doubts about how far a character of low birth can be treated as

---

[14] Ruth Perry, 'Women in Families: The Great Disinheritance', in Vivien Jones (ed.), *Women and Literature in Britain 1700–1800* (Cambridge: Cambridge University Press, 2000), 111–31 (p. 115).

an equal by those of a higher station). Even so, *The Old English Baron* can still perhaps be seen to enact for its readers a fantasy of merit overcoming the prejudice and inherited privilege represented by a figure such as Sir Robert Fitz-Owen, who remains wary that Edmund might be an impostor almost to the end. Although distinctions of rank stay in place, Edmund's character and conduct ultimately help to 'renovate' and 'reconstitute' a hierarchical society,[15] his virtues heralding the triumph of a new and more progressive social order.

Gothic Times and Manners

The location of a modern hero or heroine in a distant historical setting is a feature of many late-eighteenth- and early-nineteenth-century Gothic works that is sometimes seen to define the essentially Whiggish co-ordinates of the genre. 'Equipped with an appropriate sensibility and liberal principles', as Robert Mighall has recently argued, the heroes and heroines of Gothic fiction contend with 'the delusions and iniquities of [the past's] political and religious regime', respectively exemplified by feudal despotism and Roman Catholicism.[16] A range of prominent Gothic works might indeed be seen to stage a conflict between figures who represent modernity, the counterparts of the writer and reader, and stock villains, often libertine aristocrats or scheming priests, who stand for the forces of the past. Despite *The Old English Baron*'s apparently 'bourgeois' concern with the reward of merit and the equitable transmission of property, however, it remains difficult to see Reeve's novel in such schematic terms. As far as Reeve's representation of religion is concerned, for example, her work on the whole—notwithstanding one aside about the servants of the pre-Reformation Church (p. 14)—represents Catholicism as a given of fifteenth-century society rather than an index of any general superstition or irrationality. Whereas virtuous characters in Ann Radcliffe's fiction tend to be

---

[15] See Gary Kelly, 'Clara Reeve', *Bluestocking Feminism*, vol. vi, p. xxxii.
[16] Robert Mighall, *A Geography of Victorian Gothic Fiction: Mapping History's Nightmares* (Oxford: Oxford University Press, 1999), 9.

'honorary Protestants',[17] good characters in *The Old English Baron* are also good Catholics (Sir Philip Harclay arranges for masses to be said for the repose of a dead servant's soul, for example, and leaves money to a monastery in the will that he writes before his combat with Sir Walter Lovel). Reeve's more general construction of 'Gothic times and manners' (p. 2), like her treatment of Catholicism, is far from hostile.

As the reader is informed in the opening line, the action of *The Old English Baron* is set in the 1430s, during 'the minority of Henry the Sixth' (p. 5). Reeve's efforts to evoke the pastness of the early fifteenth century are fairly perfunctory, consisting of, for example, the detail in her account of the trial by combat, or the sub-Rowleyan inscription on the monument to Edmund's parents: 'Praye for the soules of Arthur Lord Lovele and Marie his wife, who were cut off in the flowere of their youthe' (p. 128). Despite Reeve's general inattention to customs and manners, the novel does nonetheless offer selective reference to the historical archive, with intermittent allusion to 'the glorious King Henry the Fifth' (p. 5), or to the French possessions of the English Crown gained during Henry V's reign. In the decade or so before Reeve wrote *The Old English Baron*, antiquarian scholars such as Richard Hurd, Thomas Percy, and Thomas Warton had helped to revive interest in the literary production of the Middle Ages. Following the example of Thomas Leland's historical romance *Longsword, Earl of Salisbury* (1762), set in the reign of Henry III—and praised by Euphrasia in *The Progress of Romance*— Reeve's work also paid tribute to another rapidly growing area of interest: the military exploits of England's medieval monarchs. In the year of *The Old English Baron*'s publication, and only months after the disastrous defeat at Saratoga in the American War of Independence, as Linda Colley describes in *Britons*, a group of army officers organized a lavish medieval-style tournament on the banks of the Delaware River.[18] Colley and others have

---

[17] Robert Mighall, *A Geography of Victorian Gothic Fiction*, 12.

[18] Linda Colley, *Britons: Forging the Nation, 1707–1837* (New Haven and London: Yale University Press, 1992), 147–8.

explained this resort to a national military heritage as a product of the sense of crisis which was generated by defeat in the American colonies, and exacerbated by the French Revolution and the protracted conflict with France that followed. Reeve's reference to past glories is fairly minimal, certainly in comparison with her later *Memoirs of Sir Roger de Clarendon* (1793), and contemporary readers would no doubt have been aware of the inglorious conclusion to the Hundred Years War. Even so, it is significant that Reeve's 'Gothic Story' (p. 2) evokes the Gothic for her readers in terms of an ancestral familiarity rather than a distant alterity: Edmund, the reader is told at one point, was delighted in his youth by 'histories of wars, and Knights, and Lords, and great men' (p. 53).

Reeve's work represents the contested symbol of the Gothic castle in comparably familiar, native rather than alien, terms. The castle of Otranto self-destructs at the close of Walpole's Gothic romance, just as the castle of the aristocratic villain Roderic is shown to collapse at the end of William Godwin's revision of *Otranto*, *Imogen: A Pastoral Romance, From the Ancient British* (1784). From Sophia Lee's *The Recess* (1785) onwards, moreover, many works by women writers depict the Gothic castle as a site of patriarchal coercion: Ann Radcliffe's *A Sicilian Romance* (1790), for example, adapts the motif of the haunted apartment for the purposes of a 'family secrets' plot markedly different from Reeve's, in which the heroines' mother is imprisoned by her tyrannical husband. In *The Old English Baron*, by contrast, Reeve presents the Gothic castle as the embodiment of a legitimate and venerable authority (just as William Blackstone had earlier used the metaphor of a Gothic castle as a metaphor for the accumulated authority of the English constitution[19]). The restoration of Edmund, furthermore, implicitly heralds a larger process of national reconciliation. The castle of Lovel in effect rejects or casts out the usurping Sir Walter Lovel, banished overseas and thereby purged from England, and exerts an even more

---

[19] William Blackstone, *Commentaries on the Laws of England*, 3 vols. (Oxford, 1767), iii. 268.

palpable agency in order to welcome back its rightful owner, as the servant Joseph exclaims: 'These doors open of their own accord to receive their master! This is he indeed!' (p. 115). This healing process continues as Reeve's work goes on to detail several marriages besides Edmund's, including one between Lord Graham of Scotland's 'eldest nephew' and Lord Clifford of Cumberland's 'second daughter' (p. 123). Such alliances establish significant cross-border relations, and resonantly foreshadow the emergence of a new and inclusive Britishness.[20]

Reeve helped to make the Gothic available to her contemporaries by incorporating it into a potentially revitalizing account of national identity. Instead of simply offering the reader a complacently superior and enlightened perspective on the past, therefore, *The Old English Baron* makes use of an idealized version of the medieval era in order to define the exemplary function of its romance alternative to 'real life' (p. 2). While Edmund himself is shown to be socially mobile, Reeve's work presents him against the background of a static yet harmonious system of class relations. Reeve's first title, *The Champion of Virtue*, underlines the thematic importance of the virtue that Baron Fitz-Owen and Sir Philip Harclay champion, which helps to secure general recognition of Edmund's rightful place. Reeve's second title, by contrast, *The Old English Baron*, foregrounds the status of one of the champions ahead of the merit of his protégé. (The prominent anti-Jacobin Richard Polwhele followed Reeve's example two decades later, in 1797, entitling his elegiac verse tale of rural gentry *The Old English Gentleman*.) Whether the Baron of Reeve's second title is Fitz-Owen or Sir Philip, both men are presented as benevolent paternalists who recognize the duties and obligations incumbent upon their privilege. Reeve describes fifteenth-century social relations in terms of a pre-modern 'moral economy' of landowner and tenant, as exemplified by Sir Philip Harclay's ongoing protection of his surrogate family of 'old soldiers and dependants' (p. 130). Hearing John Wyatt refer to those people 'who join in blessings and prayers to Heaven for

---

[20] Toni Wein, *British Identities, Heroic Nationalisms, and the Gothic Novel, 1764–1824* (Basingstoke: Macmillan Palgrave, 2002), 94.

their noble benefactor' Sir Philip, Edmund declares how his 'heart throbs' with the desire to imitate such 'a glorious character' (p. 73). If Edmund's virtue and sensibility seem to soften or temper the stratification of social hierarchy, the eventual revelation of his true identity nonetheless serves to legitimize—and providentially underwrite—a dyadic structure of class relations. The merit and the qualities of Edmund are never fully dissociated from his true status, indeed, since even as Edmund Twyford he is said to be possessed of something like an innate nobility: as his motto declares at the trial by combat, 'the tree is known by its fruit' (p. 87). Edmund's 'gentleness of manners', for Baron Fitz-Owen, 'distinguishes him from those of his own class' (p. 14), for example, while for Sir Philip, recognizing the 'strong resemblance' that he bears to his late friend, Edmund's qualities 'deserve that he should be placed in a higher rank' (p. 15). Characters lower down the social scale also recognize the aura of Edmund's nobility before it is officially acknowledged, such that Joseph, for example, is irresistibly drawn to the conclusion that Edmund was 'born to a higher station' (p. 21). Edmund's foster-parents only belatedly realize who he is, but they are presented as comic, even buffoonish, figures until they do, as is the case when Margery Twyford thinks she has been accused of giving birth to a bastard son. Throughout the work, domestics, servants, and peasants accept and endorse the organization of society: John Wyatt describes himself as being 'proud to wait' on Sir Philip Harclay, and the interaction between the two is characterized by their respective consciousness of 'inferiority' and 'superiority' (p. 9).

Reeve and the 1790s

The nature of Reeve's resort to 'Gothic times and manners' in *The Old English Baron* makes her engagement with *Otranto*, and her construction of romance, more complex than it might at first seem. Reeve reclaimed the gendered associations of romance in her diverse works, and drew attention to the way that feminized forms of prose fiction might contribute to the moral regulation of society.[21] Reeve's epistolary novel *The Two Mentors* (1783), for example, which deals with the education of the young ward Edward Saville, describes itself as a work 'calculated to recommend and promote the social and domestic virtues, by representing them as the only means of Happiness'; another of Reeve's novels of contemporary life, *The School for Widows* (1791), meanwhile, declares a similar purpose, seeking to counteract 'the poison of Fashion, Folly, and Dissipation'.[22] Like *The Old English Baron*, however, some of Reeve's works also offer a surplus beyond this agenda of 'feminizing' moral and social reform. Reeve's conduct-book *Plans of Education* (1792), for example, combines a discussion of improving projects in the tradition of Sarah Scott's *Millennium Hall* (1762) with a forthright polemic against the abolitionist movement (in which many other contemporary women writers were prominent). More important in the context of this introduction, Reeve's historical romance *Memoirs of Sir Roger de Clarendon* (1793) returns to the fictional setting of medieval England, and provides a fuller picture of 'the times of our Gothic ancestors'.[23]

Reeve's preface to *Sir Roger* states that 'Britain may justly boast of the great men she has produced', and presents the age of Edward III as being particularly 'fruitful of eminent men', and therefore 'an æra deserving our respect and admiration'.[24] 'When we read of our glorious ancestors', according to Reeve, asserting a continuity between past and present in familial terms, 'their actions ought to stimulate us to equal them, to support and maintain the honour of our country: to be ashamed to degenerate from our forefathers'.[25] The narrative of Reeve's title character, the 'natural son' of the Black Prince, takes in the glories of Edward

---

[21] See Gary Kelly, 'Clara Reeve', *Bluestocking Feminism*, vol. vi, p. xxx.

[22] Clara Reeve, *The Two Mentors: A Modern Story* (London, 1783), advertisement; Clara Reeve, *The School for Widows: A Novel*, 3 vols. (London, 1791), p. v.

[23] Clara Reeve, *Memoirs of Sir Roger de Clarendon, The Natural Son of Edward Prince of Wales, Commonly Called The Black Prince, with Anecdotes of Many Other Eminent Persons of the Fourteenth Century*, 3 vols. (London, 1793), i. 67.

[24] Ibid., pp. xii, xv.

[25] Ibid., p. xii.

III's reign: victory over the French at Crécy and Poitiers, the founding of the Order of the Garter, the building of St George's Chapel at Windsor, and so on. *Sir Roger* to some extent nuances its resort to the past by referring both to factional strife during the reign of Edward and to crises such as the Peasants' Revolt or the rise of Lollardy after his death. While the era evoked by Reeve is not straightforwardly harmonious, however, it still provides a critical perspective on the present: 'a true subordination of ranks and degrees was observed' at this time, Reeve's preface states, and such an example of stable hierarchy and 'good government' is said to provide the best possible antidote to 'the new philosophy of the present day'.[26] Reeve goes on briefly to acknowledge the wrongs of the old regime in France, and her reference to the revolutionaries' corruption of the 'sacred cause of liberty' (like her reference to 'degeneration', above) testifies to the ongoing influence of classical republican principles on her writing.[27] It is important, though, that *Sir Roger* gives the public spirit of great men such as the Black Prince a distinctly military inflection. If Reeve intermittently asserts the role of the social and domestic virtues in helping to maintain a united front against the French threat, *Sir Roger* also aligns itself with the masculine co-ordinates of epic history, and more specifically the bellicose rhetoric of 1790s' Loyalism.

Sir Roger de Clarendon helps to illuminate the possible meanings of Reeve's resort to the Gothic past in *The Old English Baron*, and underlines the significance of her first novel in the history of Gothic fiction. In response to the 'aristocratic' ostentation of *The Castle of Otranto*, Reeve soberly asserted the potentially reformist agency of romance, contingent upon its capacity to present what she referred to as 'the amiable side of the picture'. By emphasizing the 'pleasing features' (p. 2) of human nature in her hero Edmund, *The Old English Baron* has been seen to project both an ideology of merit and a polished masculinity back into the past, so as to prefigure and endorse the future ascendancy of 'bourgeois'

[26] Ibid., p. xvi.
[27] Ibid., iii. 225. For Reeve and classical republicanism, see Gary Kelly, 'Clara Reeve', pp. xxv, xl–xlii.

or 'feminized' values and virtues. If Reeve's preface states that
history 'too often' provides a 'melancholy retrospect' (p. 2), however, it is important that her work also locates social harmony and
stability in a historically distant era. Whereas *The Castle of
Otranto* describes the way in which the past erupts to haunt and
destabilize the present, *The Old English Baron* more straightforwardly recovers the past so as to exorcize corruption and to
confirm the legitimacy of its hero, in the process restoring a
benign and 'natural' hierarchy. Reeve's work appeared before any
larger sense of a Gothic genre was recognized, of course, and it
might therefore be regarded as an eccentric and untypical work—
the exception that proves the Gothic rule. *The Old English
Baron*'s redefinition of the Gothic past was developed further,
though, not only by Reeve's historical romance *Sir Roger de
Clarendon*, but also by a number of other fictions published in the
1790s and early 1800s. Works such as Richard Warner's *Netley
Abbey* (1795) and the anonymous *Mort Castle* (1798) similarly set
tales of usurpation, and its reversal, in an English medieval context, invoking the agency of the supernatural primarily as a
means of restoring the status quo; such works, moreover, present
their heroes as exemplary patriots who triumph over corrupt and
ambitious villains, sometimes explicitly cast as enemies of the
nation. The best-known Gothic romances of the late eighteenth
century, it is true, generally depict heroes and heroines who
struggle with the institutional forces of the past, while the best-
known women writers of Gothic fiction in this period focus primarily on the figure of the persecuted heroine. *The Old English
Baron* helps to remind us, though, that Gothic romances do not
always simply take the barbarism of the distant past as a given,
and it serves to caution against categorizing the Gothic in terms
of too narrow a range of concerns and effects. For all its initial
success, Reeve's romance is not likely to surpass *Otranto*, *The
Mysteries of Udolpho*, or *The Monk* in the favours of modern
readers. *The Old English Baron* greatly enriches our understanding of the possibilities of Gothic fiction, nonetheless, and its res-
onance belies the critical reputation it initially acquired at the
hands of Walpole and Scott as a limited, simply derivative, work.

NOTE ON THE TEXT

The text followed here is that of the revised, second edition of 1778, taken from James Trainer's 1967 edition for the Oxford English Novels series. Reeve's novel first appeared anonymously in 1777, published by W. Keymer of Colchester, under the title *The Champion of Virtue. A Gothic Story*; like the first edition of Walpole's *The Castle of Otranto*, it initially presented itself as the translation of a recovered manuscript (see Appendix 1: Reeve's 'Address to the Reader' of 1777). Encouraged by the success of *The Champion of Virtue*, Reeve prepared a new edition of her work, for which she received £10 from the London publishers Edward and Charles Dilly. Aside from the change of title, *The Old English Baron* drops *The Champion of Virtue*'s recovered manuscript framework, alters several paragraph breaks, and standardizes spelling and capitalization; it also makes general changes at the level of punctuation, reducing the use of the dash, and replacing many of the work's commas with semicolons or periods. Trainer further corrected a few obvious misprints and capitalized Father Oswald's title throughout.

Reeve prefaced the 1780 edition of her work with a fulsome dedication to Martha Bridgen, daughter of Samuel Richardson, which acknowledged the influence of her 'patronage and protection', and credited her with correcting 'the errors of the first impression': 'You took him out of this degrading dress, and encouraged him to assume a graceful and ornamental habit' (see Appendix 2). Interpreting Reeve's endorsement of these changes as proof of Bridgen's domineering influence over a first-time novelist, Jeanine Casler has called for an edition of Reeve's work that attends to her 'primary utterance', before Bridgen's involvement.[1] This demand has recently been met by Gary Kelly's edition of *The Champion of Virtue*, in the Pickering &

---

[1] Jeanine Casler, 'The Primacy of the "Rougher" Version: Neo-Conservative Editorial Practices and Clara Reeve's *The Old English Baron*', *Papers on Language and Literature*, 37 (2001), 404–37.

Chatto *Varieties of Female Gothic* collection. Kelly argues that the text of *The Champion of Virtue* is truer to the novel's 'provincial' origins, since it remains relatively unconcerned to conform to the increasingly influential standard of correct, written English.[2]

Both Casler and Kelly make a strong case for the general principle of minimal editorial intervention. In the case of *The Old English Baron*, however, there are no significant textual alterations, and the changes to punctuation and spelling arguably make the novel more accessible to the modern reader without affecting its expressive impact. Despite Bridgen's involvement in the revision process, moreover, the precise nature of the relationship between Reeve and Bridgen remains hard to quantify. Martha Bridgen was certainly an influential figure (who probably had a hand in correcting the 1801 text of her father's novel *Pamela*); Reeve, meanwhile, clearly presents herself in subservient terms in the 1780 dedication. To imply that Reeve deferred to the status of Bridgen is nonetheless perhaps to accept Walpole's or Scott's construction of her as a timid 'authoress', and to render Reeve a less autonomous figure than her allusive and wide-ranging writings suggest. Reeve surely invested in the professionalized authorial identity that Kelly argues was sought after by writers of 'correct', standard English in this period; her acceptance of the corrections made to *The Champion of Virtue* should not simply be read, therefore, as a passive or submissive act.

Aside from the fact that Reeve approved of the changes that were made to *The Old English Baron*, there are other positive reasons for keeping it as a copy-text. The most obvious of these is the pragmatic argument that *The Old English Baron* is far more widely known and quoted than *The Champion of Virtue*, having been used as the copy-text by almost every one of the many editions of Reeve's novel from 1778 onwards; it is, indeed, the text upon which her reputation as a writer of fiction largely rests. More importantly, Reeve's preface of 1778 provides a fuller and bolder statement of purpose than the 'Address to the Reader' of 1777, in effect offering a manifesto to rival Walpole's preface to

---

[2] *Varieties of Female Gothic*, ed. Gary Kelly, i: *Enlightenment Gothic and Terror Gothic* (London: Pickering & Chatto, 2002), pp. cxxi–cxxiii.

the second edition of *Otranto*. The 1777 'Address' appears relatively defensive in its dialogue with the reader ('Pray did you ever read a book called The Castle of Otranto?'), and is concerned to pre-empt objections that might be made to the novel's 'design' (see Appendix 1). The preface of 1778, by contrast, assertively announces her work as 'the literary offspring of the Castle of Otranto', and does better justice overall to the boldness and ambition of Reeve's revisionist enterprise.

SELECT BIBLIOGRAPHY

Historical and Cultural Contexts

Colley, Linda, *Britons: Forging the Nation, 1707–1837* (New Haven and London: Yale University Press, 1992).

Kliger, Samuel, *The Goths in England: A Study in Seventeenth and Eighteenth-Century Thought* (Cambridge, Mass.: Harvard University Press, 1952).

Newman, Gerald, *The Rise of English Nationalism: A Cultural History 1740–1830* (London: Weidenfeld & Nicolson, 1987).

Samuel, Raphael (ed.), *Patriotism: The Making and Unmaking of British National Identity*, 3 vols. (London: Routledge, 1989).

Critical Studies of the Gothic

Botting, Fred, *Gothic* (London: Routledge, 1996).

Brown, Marshall, 'A Philosophical View of the Gothic Novel', *Studies in Romanticism*, 26 (1987), 275–301.

Clery, E. J., *The Rise of Supernatural Fiction 1762–1800* (Cambridge: Cambridge University Press, 1995).

Duncan, Ian, *Modern Romance and Transformations of the Novel: The Gothic, Scott, Dickens* (Cambridge: Cambridge University Press, 1992).

Ellis, Kate Ferguson, *The Contested Castle: Gothic Novels and the Subversion of Domestic Ideology* (Urbana, Ill.: University of Illinois Press, 1989).

Ellis, Markman, *The History of Gothic Fiction* (Edinburgh: Edinburgh University Press, 2000).

Gamer, Michael, *Romanticism and the Gothic: Genre, Reception, and Canon Formation* (Cambridge: Cambridge University Press, 2000).

Guest, Harriet, 'The Wanton Muse: Politics and Gender in Gothic Theory after 1760', in Stephen Copley and John Whale (eds.), *Beyond Romanticism: New Approaches to Texts and Contexts 1780–1832* (London: Routledge, 1992), 118–39.

Haggerty, George E., *Gothic Fiction/Gothic Form* (University Park, Penn.: Pennsylvania State University Press, 1989).

Hogle, Jerrold E. (ed.), *The Cambridge Companion to Gothic Fiction* (Cambridge: Cambridge University Press, 2002).

Howard, Jacqueline, *Reading Gothic Fiction: A Bakhtinian Approach* (Oxford: Clarendon Press, 1994).

Howells, Coral Ann, *Love, Mystery, and Misery: Feeling in Gothic Fiction* (London: Athlone Press, 1978).

Kiely, Robert, *The Romantic Novel in England* (Cambridge, Mass.: Harvard University Press, 1972).

Kilgour, Maggie, *The Rise of the Gothic Novel* (London: Routledge, 1995).

Madoff, Mark, 'The Useful Myth of Gothic Ancestry', *Studies in Eighteenth-Century Culture*, 8 (1979), 337–50.

Mighall, Robert, *A Geography of Victorian Gothic Fiction: Mapping History's Nightmares* (Oxford: Oxford University Press, 1999).

Miles, Robert, *Gothic Writing 1750–1820: A Genealogy* (London: Routledge, 1993).

Napier, Elizabeth, *The Failure of Gothic: Problems of Disjunction in an Eighteenth-Century Literary Form* (Oxford: Clarendon Press, 1987).

Paulson, Ronald, 'Gothic Fiction and the French Revolution', *ELH* 48 (1981), 532–54.

Punter, David, *The Literature of Terror: A History of Gothic Fictions from 1765 to the Present Day* (London: Longman, 1980).

—— (ed.), *A Companion to the Gothic* (Oxford: Blackwell, 2000).

Sage, Victor, *Horror Fiction in the Protestant Tradition* (London: Macmillan, 1988).

Tompkins, J. M. S., *The Popular Novel in England, 1770–1800* (London: Constable & Co., 1932).

Watt, James, *Contesting the Gothic: Fiction, Genre, and Cultural Conflict 1764–1832* (Cambridge: Cambridge University Press, 1999).

Critical Studies of Clara Reeve and The Old English Baron

Clery, E. J., *Women's Gothic: From Clara Reeve to Mary Shelley* (Tavistock: Northcote House, 2000).

Kelly, Gary, 'Introduction: Clara Reeve', in id. (ed.), *Bluestocking Feminism: Writings of the Bluestocking Circle, 1738–1785*, vi: *Sarah Scott and Clara Reeve* (London: Pickering & Chatto, 1999).

—— 'General Introduction' and 'Introduction: Clara Reeve' in id. (ed.), *Varieties of Female Gothic*, i: *Enlightenment Gothic and Terror Gothic* (London: Pickering & Chatto, 2002).

Perry, Ruth, 'Women in Families: The Great Disinheritance', in Vivien Jones (ed.), *Women and Literature in Britain 1700–1800* (Cambridge: Cambridge University Press, 2000), 111–31.

Runge, Laura, *Gender and Language in British Literary Criticism, 1760–1790* (Cambridge: Cambridge University Press, 1997).

Wein, Toni, *British Identities, Heroic Nationalisms, and the Gothic Novel, 1764–1824* (Basingstoke: Macmillan Palgrave, 2002).

Further Reading in Oxford World's Classics

Women's Writing 1778–1838: An Anthology, ed. Fiona Robertson.

Lewis, Matthew, *The Monk*, ed. Emma McEvoy.

Radcliffe, Ann, *The Italian*, ed. Frederick Garber and E. J. Clery.

—— *The Mysteries of Udolpho*, ed. Bonamy Dobrée and Terry Castle.

—— *The Romance of the Forest*, ed. Chloe Chard.

—— *A Sicilian Romance*, ed. Alison Milbank.

Walpole, Horace, *The Castle of Otranto*, ed. W. S. Lewis and E. J. Clery.

A CHRONOLOGY OF CLARA REEVE

1791   *The School for Widows*, a three-volume novel; first volume of Tom Paine's *The Rights of Man* (1791–2); Ann Radcliffe, *The Romance of the Forest*.

1792   September Massacres in Paris followed by proclamation of Republic; Reeve, *Plans for Education; with Remarks on the Systems of other Writers*, a conduct book in the form of 'a series of Letters between Mrs Darnford and her Friends'; Mary Wollstonecraft, *A Vindication of the Rights of Woman*.

1793   Execution of Louis XVI and Marie Antoinette; France declares war on Britain; Reeve, *Memoirs of Sir Roger de Clarendon*, a three-volume historical romance set in the reign of Edward III; Charlotte Smith, *The Old Manor House*.

1794   William Godwin, *Things as They Are; or, The Adventures of Caleb Williams*; Ann Radcliffe, *The Mysteries of Udolpho*.

1796   Matthew Lewis, *The Monk*.

1797   Ann Radcliffe, *The Italian*.

1798   Irish Rebellion; first edition of S. T. Coleridge and William Wordsworth, *Lyrical Ballads*; Matthew Lewis, *The Castle Spectre*; Mary Wollstonecraft, *The Wrongs of Woman; or, Maria*.

1799   Napoleon Bonaparte becomes First Consul of France; Reeve, *Destination; or, Memoirs of a Private Family*, a three-volume novel of domestic life; *Edmond: Orphan of the Castle*, John Broster's dramatic adaptation of *The Old English Baron*.

1800   Act of Union with Ireland; second edition of *Lyrical Ballads*.

1802   Peace of Amiens brings a temporary halt to war with France; Reeve, *Edwin, King of Northumberland*, a history book for children.

1806   Charlotte Dacre, *Zofloya; or, The Moor*.

1807   Abolition of the slave trade in the British Empire; Reeve dies (3 December).

THE OLD ENGLISH BARON

A Gothic Story

PREFACE TO THE SECOND EDITION

As this Story is of a species which, tho' not new, is out of the common track, it has been thought necessary to point out some circumstances to the reader, which will elucidate the design, and, it is hoped, will induce him to form a favourable, as well as a right judgment of the work before him.

This Story is the literary offspring of the Castle of Otranto,* written upon the same plan, with a design to unite the most attractive and interesting circumstances of the ancient Romance and modern Novel, at the same time it assumes a character and manner of its own, that differs from both; it is distinguished by the appellation of a Gothic Story,* being a picture of Gothic times and manners. Fictitious Stories have been the delight of all times and all countries, by oral tradition in barbarous, by writing in more civilized ones; and altho' some persons of wit and learning have condemned them indiscriminately, I would venture to affirm, that even those who so much affect to despise them under one form, will receive and embrace them under another.

Thus, for instance, a man shall admire and almost adore the Epic poems of the Ancients, and yet despise and execrate the ancient Romances, which are only Epics in prose.*

History represents human nature as it is in real life;—alas, too often a melancholy retrospect!—Romance displays only the amiable side of the picture,* it shews the pleasing features, and throws a veil over the blemishes: Mankind are naturally pleased with what gratifies their vanity; and vanity, like all other passions of the human heart, may be rendered subservient to good and useful purposes.

I confess that it may be abused, and become an instrument to corrupt the manners and morals of mankind; so may poetry, so may plays, so may every kind of composition; but that will prove nothing more than the old saying lately revived by the philosophers the most in fashion, 'that every earthly thing has two handles.'*

The business of Romance is, first, to excite the attention; and secondly, to direct it to some useful, or at least innocent, end; Happy the writer who attains both these points, like Richardson!* and not unfortunate, or undeserving praise, he who gains only the latter, and furnishes out an entertainment for the reader!

Having, in some degree, opened my design, I beg leave to conduct my reader back again, till he comes within view of the Castle of Otranto; a work which, as already has been observed, is an attempt to unite the various merits and graces of the ancient Romance and modern Novel. To attain this end, there is required a sufficient degree of the marvellous, to excite the attention; enough of the manners of real life, to give an air of probability to the work; and enough of the pathetic, to engage the heart in its behalf.

The book we have mentioned is excellent in the two last points, but has a redundancy in the first; the opening excites the attention very strongly; the conduct of the story is artful and judicious; the characters are admirably drawn and supported; the diction polished and elegant; yet, with all these brilliant advantages, it palls upon the mind (though it does not upon the ear); and the reason is obvious, the machinery is so violent, that it destroys the effect it is intended to excite. Had the story been kept within the utmost *verge* of probability, the effect had been preserved, without losing the least circumstance that excites or detains the attention.

For instance; we can conceive, and allow of, the appearance of a ghost; we can even dispense with an enchanted sword and helmet; but then they must keep within certain limits of credibility: A sword so large as to require an hundred men to lift it; a helmet that by its own weight forces a passage through a court-yard into an arched vault, big enough for a man to go through; a picture that walks out of its frame; a skeleton ghost in a hermit's cowl.*— When your expectation is wound up to the highest pitch, these circumstances take it down with a witness, destroy the work of imagination, and, instead of attention, excite laughter. I was both surprised and vexed to find the enchantment dissolved, which I wished might continue to the end of the book; and several of its readers have confessed the same disappointment to me: The beauties are so numerous, that we cannot bear the defects, but want it to be perfect in all respects.

In the course of my observations upon this singular book, it seemed to me that it was possible to compose a work upon the same plan, wherein these defects might be avoided; and the *keeping*, as in *painting*,* might be preserved.

But then I began to fear it might happen to me as to certain translators, and imitators of Shakespeare; the unities* may be preserved, while the spirit is evaporated. However, I ventured to attempt it; I read the beginning to a circle of friends of approved judgment, and by their approbation was encouraged to proceed, and to finish it.

By the advice of the same friends I printed the first Edition in the country, where it circulated chiefly, very few copies being sent to London, and being thus encouraged, I have determined to offer a second Edition to that public which has so often rewarded the efforts of those, who have endeavoured to contribute to its entertainment.

The work has lately undergone a revision and correction, the former Edition being very incorrect;* and by the earnest solicitation of several friends, for whose judgment I have the greatest deference, I have consented to a change of the title from the *Champion of Virtue* to the *Old English Baron*:—as that character is thought to be the principal one in the story.*

I have also been prevailed upon, though with extreme reluctance, to suffer my name to appear in the title-page; and I do now, with the utmost respect and diffidence, submit the whole to the candour of the Public.

THE OLD ENGLISH BARON

A GOTHIC STORY

IN the minority of Henry the Sixth, King of England, when the renowned John Duke of Bedford was Regent of France, and Humphrey the good Duke of Gloucester was Protector of England,* a worthy Knight, called Sir Philip Harclay, returned from his travels to England, his native country. He had served under the glorious King Henry the Fifth* with distinguished valour, had acquired an honourable fame, and was no less esteemed for Christian virtues than for deeds of chivalry. After the death of his Prince, he entered into the service of the Greek Emperor,* and distinguished his courage against the encroachments of the Saracens.* In a battle there, he took prisoner a certain Gentleman, by name M. Zadisky, of Greek extraction, but brought up by a Saracen Officer; this man he converted to the Christian faith; after which he bound him to himself by the tyes of friendship and gratitude, and he resolved to continue with his Benefactor. After thirty years travel and warlike service, he determined to return to his native land, and to spend the remainder of his life in peace; and, by devoting himself to works of piety and charity, prepare for a better state hereafter.

This noble Knight had, in his early youth, contracted a strict friendship with the only son of the Lord Lovel, a gentleman of eminent virtues and accomplishments. During Sir Philip's residence in foreign countries, he had frequently written to his friend, and had for a time received answers; the last informed him of the death of old Lord Lovel, and the marriage of the young one; but from that time he had heard no more from him. Sir Philip imputed it not to neglect or forgetfulness, but to the difficulties of intercourse, common at that time to all travellers and adventurers. When he was returning home, he resolved, after looking into his family affairs, to visit the castle of Lovel, and enquire into the situation of his friend. He landed in Kent, attended by his Greek friend and two faithful servants, one of which was maimed by the wounds he had received in the defence of his Master.

Sir Philip went to his family-seat in Yorkshire; he found his mother and sister were dead, and his estates sequestered in the hands of Commissioners appointed by the Protector. He was obliged to prove the reality of his claim, and the identity of his person (by the testimony of some of the old servants of his family), after which every thing was restored to him. He took possession of his own house, established his household, settled the old servants in their former stations, and placed those he brought home in the upper offices of his family. He then left his friend to superintend his domestic affairs, and, attended by only one of his old servants, he set out for the castle of Lovel, in the west of England. They travelled by easy journeys; but, towards the evening of the second day, the servant was so ill and fatigued he could go no further; he stopped at an inn where he grew worse every hour, and the next day expired. Sir Philip was under great concern for the loss of his servant, and some for himself, being alone in a strange place; however he took courage, ordered his servant's funeral, attended it himself, and, having shed a tear of humanity over his grave, proceeded alone on his journey.

As he drew near the estate of his friend, he began to enquire of every one he met, whether the Lord Lovel resided at the seat of his ancestors? He was answered by one,—he did not know;—by another, he could not tell;—by a third, that he never heard of such a person. Sir Philip thought it strange that a man of Lord Lovel's consequence should be unknown in his own neighbourhood, and where his ancestors had usually resided. He ruminated on the uncertainty of human happiness: This world, said he, has nothing for a wise man to depend upon. I have lost all my relations, and most of my friends, and am even uncertain whether any are remaining: I will, however, be thankful for the blessings that are spared to me, and I will endeavour to replace those that I have lost. If my friend lives, he shall share my fortune with me; his children shall have the reversion of it; and I will share his comforts in return. But perhaps my friend may have met with troubles that have made him disgusted with the world: Perhaps he has buried his amiable wife, or his promising children, and, tired of public life, he is retired into a monastery. At least, I will know what all this silence means.

When he came within a mile of the Castle of Lovel, he stopped at a cottage, and asked for a draught of water: A Peasant, master of the house, brought it, and asked if his Honour would alight and take a moment's refreshment. Sir Philip accepted his offer, being resolved to make farther enquiry before he approached the castle. He asked the same questions of him, that he had before of others.—Which Lord Lovel, said the man, does your Honour enquire after?—The man whom I knew was called Arthur, said Sir Philip.—Ay, said the Peasant, he was the only surviving son of Richard Lord Lovel, as I think?—Very true, friend, he was so.—Alas, Sir, said the man, he is dead! he survived his father but a short time.—Dead! say you? how long since?—About fifteen years, to the best of my remembrance.—Sir Philip sighed deeply—alas, said he, what do we, by living long, but survive all our friends! But pray tell me how he died?—I will, Sir, to the best of my knowledge. An't please your Honour, I heard say, that he attended the King when he went against the Welch Rebels,* and he left his Lady big with child; and so there was a battle fought, and the King got the better of the Rebels: There came first a report that none of the Officers were killed; but a few days after there came a messenger with an account very different, that several were wounded, and that the Lord Lovel was slain; which sad news overset us all with sorrow, for he was a noble Gentleman, a bountiful Master, and the delight of all the neighbourhood.—He was indeed, said Sir Philip, all that is amiable and good; he was my dear and noble friend, and I am inconsolable for his loss: But the unfortunate Lady, what became of her?—Why, a'nt please your Honour, they said she died of grief for the loss of her husband; but her death was kept private for a time, and we did not know it for certain till some weeks afterwards.—The will of Heaven be obeyed! said Sir Philip; but who succeeded to the title and estate? The next heir, said the Peasant, a kinsman of the deceased, Sir Walter Lovel by name.—I have seen him, said Sir

Philip, formerly; but where was he when these events happened?—At the castle of Lovel, Sir; he came there on a visit to
the Lady, and waited there to receive my Lord, at his return from
Wales; when the news of his death arrived, Sir Walter did every
thing in his power to comfort her, and some said he was to marry
her; but she refused to be comforted, and took it so to heart that she
died.—And does the present Lord Lovel reside at the Castle?—
No, Sir.—Who then?—The Lord Baron Fitz-Owen.—And how
came Sir Walter to leave the seat of his ancestors?—Why, Sir, he
married his sister to this said Lord; and so he sold the Castle to
him, and went away, and built himself a house in the north country, as far as Northumberland, I think they call it.—That is very
strange! said Sir Philip.—So it is, please your Honour; but this is
all I know about it.—I thank you friend for your intelligence; I
have taken a long journey to no purpose, and have met with
nothing but cross accidents. This life is, indeed, a pilgrimage!
Pray direct me the nearest way to the next Monastery. Noble Sir,
said the Peasant, it is full five miles off, the night is coming on,
and the ways are bad; I am but a poor man, and cannot entertain
your Honour as you are used to; but if you will enter my poor
cottage, that, and every thing in it, are at your service. My honest
friend I thank you heartily, said Sir Philip; your kindness and
hospitality might shame many of higher birth and breeding; I will
accept your kind offer: But pray let me know the name of my
host?—John Wyatt, Sir; an honest man though a poor one, and a
Christian man, though a sinful one.—Whose cottage is this?—It
belongs to the Lord Fitz-Owen.—What family have you?—A
wife, two sons and a daughter, who will all be proud to wait upon
your Honour; let me hold your Honour's stirrup whilst you
alight. He seconded these words by the proper action, and having
assisted his guest to dismount, he conducted him into his house,
called his wife to attend him, and then led his horse under a poor
shed, that served him as a stable. Sir Philip was fatigued in body
and mind, and was glad to repose himself any where. The courtesy of his host engaged his attention, and satisfied his wishes. He
soon after returned, followed by a youth of about eighteen years;
Make haste John, said the father, and be sure you say neither

more nor less than what I have told you. I will, father, said the lad, and immediately set off, ran like a buck across the fields, and was out of sight in an instant. I hope, friend, said Sir Philip, you have not sent your son to provide for my entertainment; I am a soldier, used to lodge and fare hard; and, if it were otherwise, your courtesy and kindness would give a relish to the most ordinary food. I wish heartily, said Wyatt, it was in my power to entertain your Honour as you ought to be; but, as I cannot do so, I will, when my son returns, acquaint you with the errand I sent him on. After this they conversed together on common subjects, like fellow-creatures of the same natural form and endowments, though different kinds of education had given a conscious superiority to the one, a conscious inferiority to the other; and the due respect was paid by the latter, without being exacted by the former. In about half an hour young John returned.—Thou hast made haste, said the father. Not more than good speed, quoth the son.—Tell us, then, how you sped?—Shall I tell all that passed? said John.—All, said the father; I don't want to hide any thing. John stood with his cap in his hand, and thus told his tale.—I went straight to the Castle as fast as I could run; it was my hap to light on young Master Edmund first, so I told him just as you bad me, that a noble Gentleman was come a long journey from foreign parts to see the Lord Lovel, his friend; and, having lived abroad many years, he did not know that he was dead, and that the Castle was fallen into other hands; that upon hearing these tidings he was much grieved and disappointed, and wanting a night's lodging, to rest himself before he returned to his own home, he was fain to take up with one at our cottage; that my father thought my Lord would be angry with him, if he were not told of the stranger's journey and intentions, especially to let such a man lye at our cottage, where he could neither be lodged nor entertained according to his quality. Here John stopped, and his father exclaimed—A good lad! you did your errand very well; and tell us the answer.—John proceeded—Master Edmund ordered me some beer, and went to acquaint my Lord of the message; he stayed a while, and then came back to me. John, said he, tell the noble stranger, that the Baron Fitz-Owen greets him well, and desires him to rest assured, that though Lord Lovel is dead, and the Castle fallen into other hands, his friends will always find a welcome there; and my Lord desires that he will accept of a lodging there, while he remains in this country—so I came away directly, and made haste to deliver my errand.

Sir Philip expressed some dissatisfaction at this mark of old Wyatt's respect—I wish, said he, that you had acquainted me with your intention before you sent to inform the Baron I was here. I choose rather to lodge with you, and I propose to make amends for the trouble I shall give you. Pray, Sir, don't mention it, said the Peasant, you are as welcome as myself; I hope no offence; the only reason of my sending was, because I am both unable and unworthy to entertain your Honour.—I am sorry, said Sir Philip, you should think me so dainty; I am a Christian soldier; and him I acknowledge for my Prince and Master, accepted the invitations of the poor, and washed the feet of his disciples. Let us say no more on this head; I am resolved to stay this night in your cottage, tomorrow I will wait on the Baron, and thank him for his hospitable invitation.—That shall be as your Honour pleases, since you will condescend to stay here. John, do you run back and acquaint my Lord of it. Not so, said Sir Philip; it is now almost dark.—'Tis no matter, said John, I can go it blindfold. Sir Philip then gave him a message to the Baron in his own name, acquainting him that he would pay his respects to him in the morning. John flew back the second time, and soon returned with new commendations from the Baron, and that he would expect him on the morrow. Sir Philip gave him an angel of gold,* and praised his speed and abilities.

He supped with Wyatt and his family upon new laid eggs and rashers of bacon, with the highest relish. They praised the Creator for his gifts, and acknowledged they were unworthy of the least of his blessings. They gave the best of their two lofts up to Sir Philip, the rest of the family slept in the other, the old woman and her daughter in the bed, the father and his two sons upon clean straw. Sir Philip's bed was of a better kind, and yet much inferior to his usual accommodations; nevertheless the good

Knight slept as well in Wyatt's cottage, as he could have done in a palace.

During his sleep, many strange and incoherent dreams arose to his imagination. He thought he received a message from his friend Lord Lovel, to come to him at the Castle; that he stood at the gate and received him, that he strove to embrace him, but could not; but that he spoke to this effect.—Though I have been dead these fifteen years, I still command here, and none can enter these gates without my permission; know that it is I that invite, and bid you welcome; the hopes of my house rest upon you. Upon this he bid Sir Philip follow him; he led him through many rooms, till at last he sunk down, and Sir Philip thought he still followed him, till he came into a dark and frightful cave, where he disappeared, and in his stead he beheld a complete suit of armour stained with blood, which belonged to his friend, and he thought he heard dismal groans from beneath. Presently after, he thought he was hurried away by an invisible hand, and led into a wild heath, where the people were inclosing the ground, and making preparations for two combatants; the trumpet sounded, and a voice called out still louder, Forbear! It is not permitted to be revealed till the time is ripe for the event: Wait with patience on the decrees of Heaven.—He was then transported to his own house, where, going into an unfrequented room, he was again met by his friend, who was living, and in all the bloom of youth, as when he first knew him: He started at the sight, and awoke. The sun shone upon his curtains, and, perceiving it was day, he sat up, and recollected where he was. The images that impressed his sleeping fancy remained strongly on his mind waking; but his reason strove to disperse them; it was natural that the story he had heard should create these ideas, that they should wait on him in his sleep, and that every dream should bear some relation to his deceased friend. The sun dazzled his eyes, the birds serenaded him and diverted his attention, and a woodbine forced its way through the window, and regaled his sense of smelling with its fragrance.—He arose, paid his devotions to Heaven, and then carefully descended the narrow stairs, and went out at the door of the cottage. There he saw the industrious wife and daughter of old Wyatt at their morning work, the one milking her cow, the other feeding her poultry. He asked for a draught of milk, which, with a slice of rye bread, served to break his fast. He walked about the fields alone; for old Wyatt and his two sons were gone out to their daily labour. He was soon called back by the good woman, who told him that a servant from the Baron waited to conduct him to the Castle. He took leave of Wyatt's wife, telling her he would see her again before he left the country. The daughter fetched his horse, which he mounted, and set forward with the servant, of whom he asked many questions concerning his master's family. How long have you lived with the Baron?—Ten years.—Is he a good master?—Yes, Sir, and also a good husband and father.—What family has he?—Three sons and a daughter.—What age are they of?—The eldest son is in his seventeenth year, the second in his sixteenth, the others several years younger; but beside these my Lord has several young gentlemen brought up with his own sons, two of which are his nephews; he keeps in his house a learned clerk to teach them languages; and as for all bodily exercises, none come near them; there is a fletcher to teach them the use of the cross bow; a master to teach them to ride; another the use of the sword; another learns them to dance; and then they wrestle and run, and have such activity in all their motions, that it does one good to see them; and my Lord thinks nothing too much to bestow on their education. Truly, says Sir Philip, he does the part of a good parent, and I honour him greatly for it; but are the young gentlemen of a promising disposition?—Yes indeed, Sir, answered the servant; the young gentlemen, my Lord's sons, are hopeful youths; but yet there is one who is thought to exceed them all, though he is the son of a poor labourer.—And who is he? said the Knight.—One Edmund Twyford, the son of a cottager in our village; he is to be sure as fine a youth as ever the sun shone upon, and of so sweet a disposition that nobody envies his good fortune.—What good fortune does he enjoy?—Why, Sir, about two years ago, my Lord, at his sons request, took him into his own family, and gives him the same education as his own children; the young Lords doat upon him, especially Master William, who is about his own age: It is supposed that he will attend the young Lords when they go to the wars, which my Lord intends they shall bye and bye.—What you tell me, said Sir Philip, increases every minute my respect for your Lord; he is an excellent father and master, he seeks out merit in obscurity, he distinguishes and rewards it: I honour him with all my heart.

In this manner they conversed together till they came within view of the Castle. In a field near the house they saw a company of youths, with cross bows in their hands, shooting at a mark. There, said the servant, are our young gentlemen at their exercises. Sir Philip stopped his horse to observe them, he heard two or three of them cry out—Edmund is the victor! He wins the prize! I must, said Sir Philip, take a view of this Edmund.—He jumped off his horse, gave the bridle to the servant, and walked into the field. The young gentlemen came up, and paid their respects to him; he apologized for intruding upon their sports, and asked which was the victor? upon which the youth he spoke to beckoned to another, who immediately advanced, and made his obeisance: As he drew near, Sir Philip fixed his eyes upon him, with so much attention, that he seemed not to observe his courtesy and address. At length he recollected himself, and said, what is your name, young man?—Edmund Twyford, replied the youth; and I have the honour to attend upon the Lord Fitz-Owen's sons.—Pray, noble Sir, said the youth who first addressed Sir Philip, are not you the stranger who is expected by my father?—I am, Sir, answered he, and I go to pay my respects to him.—Will you excuse our attendance, Sir? We have not yet finished our exercises.—My dear youth, said Sir Philip, no apology is necessary; but will you favour me with your proper name, that I may know to whose courtesy I am obliged?—My name is William Fitz-Owen; that Gentleman is my eldest brother, Master Robert; that other my kinsman, Master Richard Wenlock.—Very well; I thank you, gentle Sir; I beg you not to stir another step, your servant holds my horse. Farewell, Sir, said Master William; I hope we shall have the pleasure of meeting you at dinner.—The youths returned to their sports, and Sir Philip mounted his horse and proceeded to the Castle; he entered it with a deep sigh, and melancholy recollections. The Baron received him with the utmost respect and courtesy. He gave a brief account of the principal events that had happened in the family of Lovel during his absence; he spoke of the late Lord Lovel with respect, of the present with the affection of a brother. Sir Philip, in return, gave a brief recital of his own adventures abroad, and of the disagreeable circumstances he had met with since his return home; he pathetically lamented the loss of all his friends, not forgetting that of his faithful servant on the way; saying he could be contented to give up the world, and retire to a religious house, but that he was withheld by the consideration, that some who depended entirely upon him, would want his presence and assistance; and, beside that, he thought he might be of service to many others. The Baron agreed with him in opinion, that a man was of much more service to the world who continued in it, than one who retired from it, and gave his fortune to the Church, whose servants did not always make the best use of it. Sir Philip then turned the conversation, and congratulated the Baron on his hopeful family; he praised their persons and address, and warmly applauded the care he bestowed on their education. The Baron listened with pleasure to the honest approbation of a worthy heart, and enjoyed the true happiness of a parent.

Sir Philip then made further enquiry concerning Edmund, whose appearance had struck him with an impression in his favour. That boy, said the Baron, is the son of a cottager in this neighbourhood; his uncommon merit, and gentleness of manners, distinguishes him from those of his own class; from his childhood he attracted the notice and affection of all that knew him; he was beloved every where but at his father's house, and there it should seem that his merits were his crimes; for the Peasant, his father, hated him, treated him severely, and at length threatened to turn him out of doors; he used to run here and there on errands for my people, and at length they obliged me to take notice of him; my sons earnestly desired I would take him into my family; I did so about two years ago, intending to make him their servant; but his extraordinary genius and disposition has obliged me to look upon him in a superior light; perhaps I may incur the censure of many people, by giving him so many advantages, and treating him as the companion of my children: His merit must justify, or condemn, my partiality for him; however, I trust that I have secured to my children a faithful servant of the upper kind, and an useful friend to my family. Sir Philip warmly applauded his generous host, and wished to be a sharer in his bounty to that fine youth, whose appearance indicated all the qualities that had indeared him to his companions.

At the hour of dinner the young men presented themselves before their Lord, and his guest. Sir Philip addressed himself to Edmund; he asked him many questions, and received modest and intelligent answers, and he grew every minute more pleased with him. After dinner the youths withdrew with their tutor to pursue their studies. Sir Philip sat for some time, wrapt up in meditation. After some minutes, the Baron asked him, if he might not be favoured with the fruits of his contemplations.—You shall, my Lord, answered he, for you have a right to them. I was thinking, that when many blessings are lost, we should cherish those that remain, and even endeavour to replace the others.—My Lord, I have taken a strong liking to that youth whom you call Edmund Twyford: I have neither children nor relations to claim my fortune, nor share my affections; your Lordship has many demands upon your generosity: I can provide for this promising youth without doing injustice to any one; will you give him to me?—He is a fortunate boy, said the Baron, to gain your favour so soon.— My Lord, said the Knight, I will confess to you, that the first thing that touched my heart in his favour, is a strong resemblance he bears to a certain dear friend I once had,* and his manner resembles him as much as his person; his qualities deserve that he should be placed in a higher rank; I will adopt him for my son, and introduce him into the world as my relation, if you will resign him to me: What say you?—Sir, said the Baron, you have made a noble offer, and I am too much the young man's friend to be a hindrance to his preferment. It is true that I had intended to provide for him in my own family; but I cannot do it so effectually as by giving him to you, whose generous affection being unlimited by other ties, may in time prefer him to a higher station as he shall deserve it. I have only one condition to make; that the lad shall have his option; for I would not oblige him to leave my service against his inclination.—You say well, replied Sir Philip; nor would I take him upon other terms.—Agreed then, said the Baron; let us send for Edmund hither. A servant was sent to fetch him; he came immediately, and his Lord thus bespoke him.— Edmund, you owe eternal obligations to this gentleman, who, perceiving in you a certain resemblance to a friend of his, and liking your behaviour, has taken a great affection for you, insomuch that he desires to receive you into his family: I cannot better provide for you than by disposing of you to him; and, if you have no objection, you shall return home with him when he goes from hence. The countenance of Edmund underwent many alterations during this proposal of his Lord; it expressed tenderness, gratitude, and sorrow, but the last was predominant; he bowed respectfully to the Baron and Sir Philip, and, after some hesitation, spoke as follows:—I feel very strongly the obligations I owe to this gentleman, for his noble and generous offer; I cannot express the sense I have of his goodness to me, a Peasant boy, only known to him by my Lord's kind and partial mention; this uncommon bounty claims my eternal gratitude. To you, my honoured Lord, I owe every thing, even this gentleman's good opinion—you distinguished me when nobody else did; and, next to you, your sons are my best and dearest benefactors; they introduced me to your notice. My heart is unalterably attached to this house and family, and my utmost ambition is to spend my life in your service: But if you have perceived any great and grievous faults in me, that make you wish to put me out of your family, and if you have recommended me to this gentleman in order to be rid of me, in that case I will submit to your pleasure, as I would if you should sentence me to death.

During this speech the tears made themselves channels down Edmund's cheeks; and his two noble auditors, catching the tender infection, wiped their eyes at the conclusion. My dear child, said the Baron, you overcome me by your tenderness and gratitude! I know of no faults you have committed, that I should wish to be rid of you: I thought to do you the best service by promoting you to that of Sir Philip Harclay, who is both able and willing to provide for you; but if you prefer my service to his, I will not part with you. Upon this Edmund kneeled to the Baron; he embraced his knees—My dear Lord! I am, and will be your servant, in preference to any man living; I only ask your permission to live and die in your service.—You see, Sir Philip, said the Baron, how this boy engages the heart; how can I part with him?—I cannot ask you any more, answered Sir Philip, I see it is impossible; but I esteem you both still higher than ever; the youth for his gratitude, and your Lordship for your noble mind and true generosity; blessings attend you both!—Oh, Sir, said Edmund, pressing the hand of Sir Philip, do not think me ungrateful to you, I will ever remember your goodness, and pray to Heaven to reward it; the name of Sir Philip Harclay shall be engraven upon my heart, next to my Lord and his family, for ever. Sir Philip raised the youth and embraced him, saying, if ever you want a friend, remember me; and depend upon my protection, so long as you continue to deserve it. Edmund bowed low, and withdrew, with his eyes full of tears of sensibility and gratitude. When he was gone, Sir Philip said, I am thinking, that though young Edmund wants not my assistance at present, he may hereafter stand in need of my friendship. I should not wonder if such rare qualities as he possesses, should one day create envy, and raise him enemies; in which case he might come to lose your favour, without any fault of yours or his own. I am obliged to you for the warning, said the Baron, I hope it will be unnecessary; but if ever I part with Edmund, you shall have the refusal of him. I thank your Lordship for all your civilities to me, said the Knight; I leave my best wishes with you and your hopeful family, and I humbly take my leave.—Will you not stay one night in the Castle? returned my Lord; you shall be as welcome a guest as ever.—I acknowledge your goodness and hospitality, but this house fills me with melancholy recollections; I came hither with a heavy heart, and it will not be lighter while I remain here. I shall always remember your Lordship with the highest respect and esteem; and I pray God to preserve you, and increase your blessings!

After some further ceremonies, Sir Philip departed, and returned to old Wyatt's, ruminating on the vicissitude of human affairs, and thinking on the changes he had seen.

At his return to Wyatt's cottage, he found the family assembled together. He told them he would take another night's lodging there, which they heard with great pleasure; for he had familiarised himself to them in the last evening's conversation, insomuch that they began to enjoy his company. He told Wyatt of the misfortune he had sustained by losing his servant on the way, and wished he could get one to attend him home in his place. Young John looked earnestly at his father, who returned a look of approbation. I perceive one in this company, said he, that would be proud to serve your Honour; but I fear he is not brought up well enough. John coloured with impatience, he could not forbear speaking. Sir, I can answer for an honest heart, a willing mind, and a light pair of heels; and though I am somewhat aukward, I shall be proud to learn, to please my noble Master, if he will but try me. You say well, said Sir Philip, I have observed your qualifications, and if you are desirous to serve me, I am equally pleased with you; if your father has no objection I will take you. Objection, Sir! said the old man; it will be my pride to prefer him to such a noble gentleman; I will make no terms for him, but leave it to your Honour to do for him as he shall deserve. Very well, said Sir Philip, you shall be no loser by that; I will charge myself with the care of the young man. The bargain was struck, and Sir Philip purchased a horse for John of the old man. The next morning they set out; the Knight left marks of his bounty with the good couple, and departed, laden with their blessing and prayers. He stopped at the place where his faithful servant was buried, and caused masses to be said for the repose of his soul; then, pursuing his way by easy journeys, arrived in safety at home. His family rejoiced at his return; he settled his new servant in attendance upon his person; he then looked round his neighbourhood for objects of his charity; when he saw merit in distress, it was his delight to raise and support it: He spent his time in the service of his Creator, and glorified him in doing good to his creatures. He reflected frequently upon every thing that had befallen him in his

late journey to the west; and, at his leisure, took down all the
particulars in writing.

Here follows an interval of four years, as by the manuscript;*
and this omission seems intended by the Writer. What follows is in a
different hand, and the character is more modern.

ABOUT this time the prognosticks* of Sir Philip Harclay began to
be verified, that Edmund's good qualities might one day excite
envy and create him enemies. The sons and kinsmen of his patron
began to seek occasion to find fault with him, and to depreciate
him with others. The Baron's eldest son and heir, Master Robert,
had several contests with Master William, the second son, upon
his account: This youth had a warm affection for Edmund, and
whenever his brother and kinsmen treated him slightly, he supported him against their malicious insinuations. Mr. Richard
Wenlock, and Mr. John Markham, were the sisters sons of the
Lord Fitz-Owen; and there were several other more distant relations, who, with them, secretly envied Edmund's fine qualities,
and strove to lessen him in the esteem of the Baron and his family.
By degrees they excited a dislike in Master Robert, that in time
was fixed into habit, and fell little short of aversion.

Young Wenlock's hatred was confirmed by an additional
circumstance: He had a growing passion for the Lady Emma, the
Baron's only daughter; and, as love is eagle-eyed, he saw, or
fancied he saw her cast an eye of preference on Edmund. An
accidental service that she received from him, had excited her
grateful regards and attentions towards him. The incessant view
of his fine person and qualities, had perhaps improved her esteem
into a still softer sensation, though she was yet ignorant of it, and
thought it only the tribute due to gratitude and friendship.

One Christmas time, the Baron and all his family went to visit a
family in Wales; crossing a ford, the horse that carried the Lady
Emma, who rode behind her cousin Wenlock, stumbled and fell
down, and threw her off into the water: Edmund dismounted in a
moment, and flew to her assistance; he took her out so quick, that
the accident was not known to some part of the company. From

this time Wenlock strove to undermine Edmund in her esteem, and she conceived herself obliged in justice and gratitude to defend him against the malicious insinuations of his enemies. She one day asked Wenlock, why he in particular should endeavour to recommend himself to her favour, by speaking against Edmund, to whom she was under great obligations?—He made but little reply; but the impression sunk deep into his rancorous heart; every word in Edmund's behalf was like a poisoned arrow that rankled in the wound, and grew every day more inflamed. Sometimes he would pretend to extenuate Edmund's supposed faults, in order to load him with the sin of ingratitude upon other occasions. Rancour works deepest in the heart that strives to conceal it; and, when covered by art, frequently puts on the appearance of candour. By these means did Wenlock and Markham impose upon the credulity of Master Robert and their other relations: Master William only stood proof against all their insinuations.

The same autumn that Edmund compleated his eighteenth year, the Baron declared his intention of sending the young men of his house to France the following spring, to learn the art of war,* and signalize their courage and abilities.

Their ill-will towards Edmund was so well concealed, that his patron had not discovered it; but it was whispered among the servants, who are generally close observers of the manners of their principals. Edmund was a favourite with them all, which was a strong presumption that he deserved to be so, for they seldom shew much regard to dependents, or to superiour domestics, who are generally objects of envy and dislike. Edmund was courteous, but not familiar with them; and, by this means, gained their affections without soliciting them. Among them was an old serving man, called Joseph Howell; this man had formerly served the old Lord Lovel, and his son; and when the young Lord died, and Sir Walter sold the castle to his brother-in-law, the Lord Fitz-Owen, he only of all the old servants was left in the house, to take care of it, and to deliver it into the possession of the new proprietor, who retained him in his service: He was a man of few words but much reflection; and without troubling himself about other people's affairs, went silently and properly about his own business; more solicitous to discharge his duty, than to recommend himself to notice, and not seeming to aspire to any higher office than that of a serving man. This old man would fix his eyes upon Edmund, whenever he could do it without observation; sometimes he would sigh deeply, and a tear would start from his eye, which he strove to conceal from observation. One day Edmund surprized him in this tender emotion, as he was wiping his eyes with the back of his hand: Why, said he, my good friend, do you look at me so earnestly and affectionately?—Because I love you Master Edmund, said he, because I wish you well.—I thank you kindly, answered Edmund; I am unable to repay your love, otherwise than by returning it, which I do sincerely.—I thank you, Sir, said the old man; that is all I desire, and more than I deserve.—Do not say so, said Edmund; if I had any better way to thank you, I would not say so much about it; but words are all my inheritance. Upon this he shook hands with Joseph, who withdrew hastily to conceal his emotion, saying, God bless you Master, and make your fortune equal to your deserts! I cannot help thinking you were born to a higher station than what you now hold:—You know to the contrary, said Edmund; but Joseph was gone out of sight and hearing.

The notice and observation of strangers, and the affection of individuals, together with that inward consciousness that always attends superiour qualities, would sometimes kindle the flames of ambition in Edmund's heart; but he checked them presently by reflecting upon his low birth and dependant station. He was modest, yet intrepid; gentle and courteous to all; frank and unreserved to those that loved him, discreet and complaisant to those who hated him; generous and compassionate to the distresses of his fellow-creatures in general; humble, but not servile, to his patron and superiors. Once, when he with a manly spirit justified himself against a malicious imputation, his young Lord, Robert, taxed him with pride and arrogance to his kinsmen. Edmund denied the charge against him with equal spirit and modesty. Master Robert answered him sharply—How dare you contradict my cousins! do you mean to give them the lye?—Not in words Sir, said Edmund; but I will behave so as that you shall not believe them. Master Robert haughtily bade him be silent and know himself, and not presume to contend with men so much his superiors in every respect. These heart-burnings in some degree subsided by their preparations for going to France. Master Robert was to be presented at court before his departure, and it was expected that he should be knighted. The Baron designed Edmund to be his Esquire; but this was frustrated by his old enemies, who persuaded Robert to make choice of one of his own domestics, called Thomas Hewson; him did they set up as a rival to Edmund, and he took every occasion to affront him. All that Master Robert gained by this step, was the contempt of those who saw Edmund's merit, and thought it want of discernment in him not to distinguish and reward it.—Edmund requested of his Lord that he might be Master William's attendant; and when, said he, my patron shall be knighted, as I make no doubt he will one day be, he has promised that I shall be his Esquire. The Baron granted Edmund's request; and, being freed from servitude to the rest, he was devoted to that of his beloved Master William, who treated him in public as his principal domestic, but in private as his chosen friend and brother.

The whole cabal* of his enemies consulted together in what manner they should vent their resentment against him; and it was agreed that they should treat him with indifference and neglect, till they should arrive in France; and when there, they should contrive to render his courage suspected, and by putting him upon some desperate enterprize, rid themselves of him for ever. About this time died the great Duke of Bedford,* to the irreparable loss of the English nation. He was succeeded by Richard Plantagenet, Duke of York,* as Regent of France, of which great part had revolted to Charles the Dauphin.* Frequent actions ensued. Cities were lost and won, and continual occasions offered to exercise the courage and abilities of the youth of both nations.

The young men of Baron Fitz-Owen's house were recommended particularly to the Regent's notice. Master Robert was knighted, with several other young men of family who distinguished themselves by their spirit and activity upon every occasion. The youth were daily employed in warlike exercises, and frequent actions; and made their first essay in arms in such a manner as to bring into notice all that deserved it.

Various arts were used by Edmund's enemies to expose him to danger; but all their contrivances recoiled upon themselves, and brought increase of honour upon Edmund's head: He distinguished himself upon so many occasions, that Sir Robert himself began to pay him more than ordinary regard, to the infinite mortification of his kinsmen and relations. They laid many schemes against him, but none took effect.

From this place the characters in the manuscript are effaced by time and damp. Here and there some sentences are legible, but not sufficient to pursue the thread of the story. Mention is made of several actions in which the young men were engaged—that Edmund distinguished himself by intrepidity in action; by gentleness, humanity and modesty in the cessations—that he attracted the notice of every person of observation, and also that he received personal commendation from the Regent.

The following incidents are clear enough to be transcribed; but the beginning of the next succeeding pages is obliterated: However, we may guess at the beginning by what remains.

* * * * * * * * * * * * * * * *

As soon as the cabal met in Sir Robert's tent, Mr. Wenlock thus began. You see, my friends, that every attempt we make to humble this upstart, turns into applause, and serves only to raise his pride still higher. Something must be done, or his praise will go home before us, at our own expence; and we shall seem only foils to set off his glories. Any thing would I give to the man who should execute our vengeance upon him. Stop there, cousin Wenlock, said Sir Robert; though I think Edmund proud and vainglorious, and would join in any scheme to humble him, and make him know himself, I will not suffer any man to use such base methods to effect it. Edmund is brave; and it is beneath an Englishman to revenge himself by unworthy means; if any such are used, I will be the first man to bring the guilty to justice; and if I hear another word to this purpose, I will inform my brother William, who will acquaint Edmund with your mean intentions. Upon this the cabal drew back, and Mr. Wenlock protested that he meant no more than to mortify his pride, and make him know his proper station. Soon after Sir Robert withdrew, and they resumed their deliberations.

Then spoke Thomas Hewson: There is a party to be sent out to-morrow night, to intercept a convoy of provisions for the relief of Rouen; I will provoke Mr. Edmund to make one of this party, and when he is engaged in the action, I and my companions will draw off, and leave him to the enemy, who I trust will so handle him, that you shall no more be troubled with him. This will do, said Mr. Wenlock; but let it be kept from my two cousins and only known to ourselves; if they offer to be of the party, I will persuade them off it: And you, Thomas, if you bring this scheme to a conclusion, may depend upon my eternal gratitude.—And mine, said Markham; and so said all. The next day the affair was publickly mentioned; and Hewson, as he promised, provoked Edmund to the trial: Several young men of family offered themselves; among the rest, Sir Robert, and his brother William. Mr. Wenlock persuaded them not to go, and set the danger of the enterprize in the strongest colours. At last Sir Robert complained of the tooth-ach, and was confined to his tent; Edmund waited on him; and judging by the ardour of his own courage of that of his patron, thus bespoke him. I am greatly concerned dear Sir, that we cannot have your company at night; but as I know what you will suffer in being absent, I would beg the favour of you to let me use your arms and device, and I will promise not to disgrace them. No, Edmund, I cannot consent to that: I thank you for your noble offer, and will remember it to your advantage; but I cannot wear honours of another man's getting. You have awakened me to a sense of my duty: I will go with you, and contend with you for glory; and William shall do the same.

In a few hours they were ready to set out. Wenlock and Markham, and their dependants, found themselves engaged in honour to go upon an enterprize they never intended; and set out, with heavy hearts, to join the party. They marched in silence in the horrors of a dark night, and wet roads; they met the convoy where they expected, and a sharp engagement ensued. The victory was some time doubtful; but the moon rising on the backs of the English, gave them the advantage. They saw the disposition of their enemies, and availed themselves of it. Edmund advanced the foremost of the party; he drew out the leader on the French side; he slew him. Mr. William pressed forward to assist his friend, Sir Robert, to defend his brother; Wenlock, and Markham, from shame to stay behind.

Thomas Hewson and his associates drew back on their side; the French perceived it, and pursued the advantage. Edmund pushed them in front; the young nobles all followed him; they broke through the detachment, and stopped the waggons. The officer who commanded the party, encouraged them to go on; the defeat was soon compleat, and the provisions carried in triumph to the English camp.

Edmund was presented to the Regent as the man to whom the victory was chiefly owing. Not a tongue presumed to move itself against him; even malice and envy were silenced.

Approach, young man, said the Regent, that I may confer upon you the honour of knighthood, which you have well deserved. Mr. Wenlock could no longer forbear speaking: Knighthood, said he, is an order belonging to gentlemen, it cannot be conferred on a peasant. What say you, Sir! returned the Regent; is this youth a peasant?—He is, said Wenlock; let him deny it if he can. Edmund, with a modest bow, replied, It is true indeed I am a peasant, and this honour is too great for me: I have only done my duty. The Duke of York, whose pride of birth equalled that of any man living or dead, sheathed his sword immediately. Though, said he, I cannot reward you as I intended, I will take care that you shall have a large share in the spoils of this night; and, I declare publickly, that you stand first in the list of gallant men in this engagement.

Thomas Hewson and his associates made a poor figure in their return; they were publickly reproved for their backwardness. Hewson was wounded in body and more in mind, for the bad success of his ill laid design. He could not hold up his head before

Edmund; who, unconscious of their malice, administered every kind of comfort to them. He spoke in their behalf to the commanding officer, imputing their conduct to unavoidable accidents. He visited them privately; he gave them a part of the spoils allotted to himself; by every act of valour and courtesy he strove to engage those hearts that hated, envied, and maligned him: But where hatred arises from envy of superior qualities, every display of those qualities increases the cause from whence it arises.

Another pause ensues here.

The young nobles and gentlemen who distinguished Edmund, were prevented from raising him to preferment by the insinuations of Wenlock and his associates, who never failed to set before them his low descent, and his pride and arrogance in presuming to rank with gentlemen.

Here the manuscript is not legible for several pages. There is mention, about this time, of the death of the Lady Fitz-Owen, but not the cause.

Wenlock rejoiced to find that his schemes took effect, and that they should be recalled at the approach of winter. The Baron was glad of a pretence to send for them home; for he could no longer endure the absence of his children, after the loss of their mother.

The manuscript is again defaced for many leaves; at length the letters become more legible, and the remainder of it is quite perfect.

FROM the time the young men returned from France, the enemies of Edmund employed their utmost abilities to ruin him in the Baron's opinion, and get him dismissed from the family. They insinuated a thousand things against him that happened, as they said, during his residence in France, and therefore could not be known to his master; but when the Baron privately enquired of his two elder sons, he found there was no truth in their reports. Sir Robert, though he did not love him, scorned to join in untruths against him. Mr. William spoke of him with the warmth of fraternal affection. The Baron perceived that his kinsmen disliked Edmund; but his own good heart hindered him from seeing the baseness of theirs. It is said that continual dropping will wear away a stone; so did their incessant reports, by insensible degrees, produce a coolness in his patron's behaviour towards him. If he behaved with manly spirit, it was misconstrued into pride and arrogance; his generosity was imprudence; his humility was hypocrisy, the better to cover his ambition. Edmund bore patiently all the indignities that were thrown upon him; and, though he felt them severely in his bosom, scorned to justify his conduct at the expence even of his enemies. Perhaps his gentle spirit might at length have sunk under this treatment, but providence interposed in his behalf; and, by seemingly accidental circumstances, conducted him imperceptibly towards the crisis of his fate.

Father Oswald, who had been preceptor to the young men, had a strong affection for Edmund, from a thorough knowledge of his heart; he saw through the mean artifices that were used to undermine him in his patron's favour; he watched their machinations, and strove to frustrate their designs.

This good man used frequently to walk out with Edmund; they conversed upon various subjects; and the youth would lament to him the unhappiness of his situation, and the peculiar circumstances that attended him. The Father, by his wholesome advice, comforted his drooping heart; and confirmed him in his resolution of bearing unavoidable evils with patience and fortitude, from the consciousness of his own innocence, and the assurance of a future and eternal reward.

One day, as they were walking in a wood near the castle,

Edmund asked the Father what meant those preparations for building, the cutting down trees and burning of bricks?—What, said Oswald, have not you heard that my Lord is going to build a new apartment on the west side of the castle?—And why, said Edmund, should my Lord be at that expence when there is one on the east side that is never occupied?—That apartment, said the friar, you must have observed is always shut up. I have observed it often, said Edmund; but I never presumed to ask any questions about it.—You had then, said Oswald, less curiosity and more discretion than is common at your age.—You have raised my curiosity, said Edmund; and, if it be not improper, I beg of you to gratify it.—We are alone, said Oswald, and I am so well assured of your prudence, that I will explain this mystery in some degree to you.

You must know, that apartment was occupied by the last Lord Lovel when he was a batchelor. He married in his father's life-time, who gave up his own apartment to him, and offered to retire to this himself; but the son would not permit him, he chose to sleep here, rather than in any other. He had been married about three months when his father, the old Lord, died of a fever. About twelve months after his marriage, he was called upon to attend the King, Henry the Fourth,* on an expedition into Wales, whither he was attended by many of his dependants. He left his lady big with child, and full of care and anxiety for his safety and return.

After the King had chastised the Rebels, and obtained the victory, the Lord Lovel was expected home every day; various reports were sent home before him; one messenger brought an account of his health and safety—soon after another came with bad news, that he was slain in battle. His kinsman, Sir Walter Lovel, came here on a visit to comfort the Lady; and he waited to receive his kinsman at his return. It was he that brought the news of the sad event of the battle to the Lady Lovel.

She fainted away at the relation; but, when she revived, exerted the utmost resolution; saying, it was her duty to bear this dreadful stroke with Christian fortitude and patience, especially in regard to the child she went with, the last remains of her beloved husband, and the undoubted heir of a noble house. For several days she seemed an example of patience and resignation; but then, all at once, she renounced them, and broke out into passionate and frantic exclamations; she said, that her dear Lord was basely murdered; that his ghost had appeared to her, and revealed his fate: She called upon Heaven and earth to revenge her wrongs; saying, she would never cease complaining to God, and the King, for vengeance and justice.

Upon this, Sir Walter told the servants that Lady Lovel was distracted, from grief for the death of her Lord; that his regard for her was as strong as ever; and that, if she recovered, he would himself be her comforter, and marry her. In the mean time she was confined in this very apartment, and in less than a month the poor Lady died.—She lies buried in the family vault in St. Austin's church* in the village. Sir Walter took possession of the Castle, and all the other estates, and assumed the title of Lord Lovel.

Soon after, it was reported that the Castle was haunted, and that the ghosts of Lord and Lady Lovel had been seen by several of the servants. Whoever went into this apartment were terrified by uncommon noises and strange appearances; at length this apartment was wholly shut up, and the servants were forbid to enter it, or to talk of any thing relating to it: However, the story did not stop here; it was whispered about, that the new Lord Lovel was so disturbed every night that he could not sleep in quiet; and, being at last tired of the place, he sold the Castle and estate of his ancestors, to his brother-in-law the Lord Fitz-Owen, who now enjoys it, and left this country.

All this is news to me, said Edmund; but, Father, tell me what grounds there were for the Lady's suspicion that her Lord died unfairly.—Alas! said Oswald, that is only known to God. There were strange thoughts in the minds of many at that time; I had mine; but I will not disclose them, not even to you. I will not injure those who may be innocent; and I leave it to Providence, who will doubtless, in its own best time and manner, punish the guilty. But let what I have told you be as if you had never heard it.

I thank you for these marks of your esteem and confidence, said

Edmund; be assured that I will not abuse them; nor do I desire to pry into secrets not proper to be revealed: I entirely approve your discretion, and acquiesce in your conclusion, that Providence will in its own time vindicate its ways to man: If it were not for that trust, my situation would be insupportable. I strive earnestly to deserve the esteem and favour of good men; I endeavour to regulate my conduct so as to avoid giving offence to any man; but I see, with infinite pain, that it is impossible for me to gain these points.—I see it too, with great concern, said Oswald; and every thing that I can say and do in your favour is misconstrued; and, by seeking to do you service, I lose my own influence: But I will never give my sanction to acts of injustice, nor join to oppress innocence. My dear child, put your trust in God: He who brought light out of darkness, can bring good out of evil.—I hope and trust so, said Edmund; but, Father, if my enemies should prevail, if my Lord should believe their stories against me, and I should be put out of the house with disgrace, what will become of me? I have nothing but my character to depend upon; if I lose that, I lose every thing; and I see they seek no less than my ruin.—Trust in my Lord's honour and justice, replied Oswald; he knows your virtue, and he is not ignorant of their ill-will towards you.—I know my Lord's justice too well to doubt it, said Edmund; but would it not be better to rid him of this trouble, and his family of an incumbrance? I would gladly do something for myself, but cannot without my Lord's recommendation; and such is my situation, that I fear the asking for a dismission would be accounted base ingratitude: Beside, when I think of leaving this house, my heart saddens at the thought, and tells me I cannot be happy out of it: Yet I think I could return to a peasant's life with chearfulness, rather than live in a palace under disdain and contempt.—Have patience a little longer, my son, said Oswald; I will think of some way to serve you, and to represent your grievances to my Lord, without offence to either: Perhaps the causes may be removed. Continue to observe the same irreproachable conduct; and be assured that Heaven will defend your innocence, and defeat the unjust designs of your enemies. Let us now return home.

About a week after this conference, Edmund walked out in the fields ruminating on the disagreeable circumstances of his situation. Insensible of the time, he had been out several hours without perceiving how the day wore away, when he heard himself called by name several times; looking backward he saw his friend Mr. William, and hallowed to him. He came running towards him; and, leaping over the style, stood still a while to recover his breath. What is the matter, Sir, said Edmund? your looks bespeak some tidings of importance. With a look of tender concern and affection, the youth pressed his hand and spoke. My dear Edmund, you must come home with me directly; your old enemies have united to ruin you with my father; my brother Robert has declared that he thinks there will be no peace in our family till you are dismissed from it, and told my father, he hoped he would not break with his kinsmen rather than give up Edmund.—But what do they lay to my charge? said Edmund.—I cannot rightly understand, answered William, for they make a great mystery of it; something of great consequence they say; but they will not tell me what: However, my father has told them that they must bring their accusation before your face, and he will have you answer them publicly. I have been seeking you this hour, to inform you of this, that you might be prepared to defend yourself against your accusers.—God reward you, Sir, said Edmund, for all your goodness to me! I see they are determined to ruin me if possible: I shall be compelled to leave the Castle; but, whatever becomes of me, be assured you shall have no cause to blush for your kindness and partiality to your Edmund.—I know it, I am sure of it, said William; and here I swear to you, as Jonathan did to David,* I beseech Heaven to bless me, as my friendship to you shall be steady and inviolable!—Only so long as I shall deserve so great a blessing, interrupted Edmund.—I know your worth and honour, continued William; and such is my confidence in your merit, that I firmly believe Heaven designs you for something extraordinary; and I expect that some great and unforeseen event will raise you to the rank and station to which you appear to belong: Promise me, therefore, that whatever may be your fate you will preserve the same friendship for me that I bear to you.—Edmund was so much affected that he could not answer but in broken sentences. Oh my friend, my master! I vow, I promise, my heart promises!—He kneeled down with clasped hands, and uplifted eyes: William kneeled by him, and they invoked the Supreme to witness to their friendship, and implored his blessing upon it: They then rose up and embraced each other, while tears of cordial affection bedewed their cheeks.

As soon as they were able to speak, Edmund conjured his friend not to expose himself to the displeasure of his family out of kindness to him. I submit to the will of Heaven, said he, I wait with patience its disposal of me; if I leave the Castle I will find means to inform you of my fate and fortunes.—I hope, said William, that things may yet be accommodated; but do not take any resolution, let us act as occasions arise.

In this manner these amiable youths conferred, till they arrived at the Castle. The Baron was sitting in the great hall on a high chair with a footstep before, with the state and dignity of a judge; before him stood Father Oswald, as pleading the cause for himself and Edmund. Round the Baron's chair stood his eldest son and his kinsmen, with their principal domestics. The old servant, Joseph, at some distance, with his head leaning forward, as listening with the utmost attention to what passed. Mr. William approached the chair.—My Lord, I have found Edmund, and brought him to answer for himself.—You have done well, said the Baron. Edmund, come hither; you are charged with some indiscretions, for I cannot properly call them crimes: I am resolved to do justice between you and your accusers; I shall therefore hear you as well as them; for no man ought to be condemned unheard.—My Lord, said Edmund, with equal modesty and intrepidity, I demand my trial; if I shall be found guilty of any crimes against my Benefactor, let me be punished with the utmost rigor: But if, as I trust, no such charge can be proved against me, I know your goodness too well to doubt that you will do justice to me, as well as to others; and if it should so happen that by the misrepresentations of my enemies (who have long sought my ruin privately, and now avow it publicly), if by their artifices your Lordship should be induced to think me guilty, I would submit to your sentence in silence, and appeal to another tribunal.—See, said Mr. Wenlock, the confidence of the fellow! he already supposes that my Lord must be in the wrong if he condemns him; and then this meek creature will appeal to another tribunal: To whose will he appeal? I desire he may be made to explain himself.—That I will immediately, said Edmund, without being compelled; I only meant to appeal to Heaven that best knows my innocence.—'Tis true, said the Baron, and no offence to any one; man can only judge by appearances, but Heaven knows the heart: Let every one of you bear this in mind, that you may not bring a false accusation, nor justify yourselves by concealing the truth. Edmund, I am informed that Oswald and you have made very free with me and my family in some of your conversations; you were heard to censure me for the absurdity of building a new apartment on the west side of the Castle when there was one on the east side uninhabited: Oswald said, that apartment was shut up because it was haunted; that some shocking murther had been committed there; adding many particulars concerning Lord Lovel's family, such as he could not know the truth of, and if he had known, was imprudent to reveal. But further, you complained of ill treatment here; and mentioned an intention to leave the Castle, and seek your fortune elsewhere. I shall examine into all these particulars in turn. At present I desire you, Edmund, to relate all that you can remember of the conversation that passed between you and Oswald in the wood last Monday.—Good God! said Edmund, is it possible that any person could put such a construction upon so innocent a conversation?

Tell me then, said the Baron, the particulars of it.—I will, my Lord, as nearly as my memory will allow me. Accordingly he related most of the conversation that passed in the wood; but, in the part that concerned the family of Lovel, he abbreviated as much as possible. Oswald's countenance cleared up, for he had done the same before Edmund came. The Baron called to his eldest son,—You hear, Sir Robert, what both parties say: I have questioned them separately; neither of them knew what the other would answer, yet their accounts agree almost to a word.—I confess they do so, answered Sir Robert; but, Sir, it is very bold and presuming for them to speak of our family affairs in such a manner; if my uncle, Lord Lovel, should come to know it, he would punish them severely; and, if his honour is reflected upon, it becomes us to resent and to punish it. Here Mr. Wenlock broke out into passion, and offered to swear to the truth of his accusation. Be silent, Dick, said the Baron; I shall judge for myself. I protest, said he to Sir Robert, I never heard so much as Oswald has now told me concerning the deaths of Lord and Lady Lovel; I think it is best to let such stories alone till they die away of themselves. I had, indeed, heard of an idle story of the east apartments being haunted when first I came hither, and my brother advised me to shut it up till it should be forgotten; but what has now been said, has suggested a thought that may make that apartment useful in future. I have thought of a punishment for Edmund that will stop the mouth of his accusers for the present; and, as I hope, will establish his credit with every body. Edmund will you undertake this adventure for me?—What adventure, my Lord, said Edmund? There is nothing I would not undertake to show my gratitude and fidelity to you. As to my courage, I would shew that at the expence of my malicious accusers, if respect to my Lord's blood did not tie up my hands; as I am situated I beg it may be put to the proof in whatever way is most for my master's service.—That is well said, cried the Baron: As to your enemies, I am thinking how to separate you from them effectually; of that I shall speak hereafter. I am going to try Edmund's courage; he shall sleep three nights in the east apartment, that he may testify to all whether it be haunted or not; afterwards I will have that apartment set in order, and my eldest son shall take it for his own; it will spare me some expence, and answer my purpose as well, or better: Will you consent Edmund?—With all my heart, my Lord, said Edmund, I have not wilfully offended God or man; I have, therefore, nothing to fear.—Brave boy! said my Lord; I am not deceived in you, nor shall you be deceived in your reliance on me. You shall sleep in that apartment to-night, and to-morrow I will have some private talk with you. Do you, Oswald, go with me; I want to have some conversation with you. The rest of you, retire to your studies and business; I will meet you at dinner.

Edmund retired to his own chamber, and Oswald was shut up with the Baron; he defended Edmund's cause and his own, and laid open as much as he knew of the malice and designs of his enemies. The Baron expressed much concern at the untimely deaths of Lord and Lady Lovel, and desired Oswald to be circumspect in regard to what he had to say of the circumstances attending them; adding, that he was both innocent and ignorant of any treachery towards either of them. Oswald excused himself for his communications to Edmund, saying, they fell undesignedly into the subject, and that he mentioned it in confidence to him only.

The Baron sent orders to the young men to come to dinner; but they refused to meet Edmund at table; accordingly he ate in the steward's apartment. After dinner the Baron tried to reconcile his kinsmen to Edmund; but found it impossible. They saw their designs were laid open; and judging of him by themselves, thought it impossible to forgive or be forgiven. The Baron ordered them to keep in separate apartments; he took his eldest son for his own companion, as being the most reasonable of the malecontents, and ordered his kinsmen to keep their own apartment, with a servant to watch their motions. Mr. William had Oswald for his companion. Old Joseph was bid to attend on Edmund; to serve him at supper; and, at the hour of nine, to conduct him to the haunted apartment. Edmund desired that he might have a light and his sword, lest his enemies should endeavour to surprise him. The Baron thought his request reasonable, and complied with it.

There was a great search to find the key of the apartment; at last it was discovered by Edmund himself among a parcel of old rusty keys in a lumber room. The Baron sent the young men their suppers to their respective apartments. Edmund declined eating, and desired to be conducted to his apartment. He was accompanied by most of the servants to the door of it; they wished him success, and prayed for him as if he had been going to execution.

The door was with great difficulty unlocked, and Joseph gave

Edmund a lighted lamp, and wished him a good night; he returned his good wishes to them all with the utmost chearfulness, took the key on the inside of the door, and dismissed them.

He then took a survey of his chamber; the furniture, by long neglect, was decayed and dropping to pieces; the bed was devoured by the moths, and occupied by the rats, who had built their nests there with impunity for many generations. The bedding was very damp, for the rain had forced its way through the ceiling; he determined, therefore, to lie down in his clothes. There were two doors on the further side of the room with keys in them; being not at all sleepy, he resolved to examine them; he attempted one lock, and opened it with ease; he went into a large dining-room, the furniture of which was in the same tattered condition; out of this was a large closet with some books in it, and hung round with coats of arms, with genealogies and alliances of the house of Lovel; he amused himself here some minutes, and then returned into the bed-chamber.

He recollected the other door, and resolved to see where it led to; the key was rusted into the lock, and resisted his attempts; he set the lamp on the ground, and exerting all his strength opened the door, and at the same instant the wind of it blew out the lamp, and left him in utter darkness. At the same moment he heard a hollow rustling noise like that of a person coming through a narrow passage. Till this moment not one idea of fear had approached the mind of Edmund; but just then, all the concurrent circumstances of his situation struck upon his heart, and gave him a new and disagreeable sensation. He paused a while; and, recollecting himself, cried out aloud—What should I fear? I have not wilfully offended God, or man; why, then, should I doubt protection? But I have not yet implored the divine assistance; how then can I expect it! Upon this, he kneeled down and prayed earnestly, resigning himself wholly to the will of Heaven; while he was yet speaking, his courage returned, and he resumed his usual confidence; again he approached the door from whence the noise proceeded; he thought he saw a glimmering light upon a staircase before him. If, said he, this apartment is haunted, I will use my endeavours to discover the cause of it; and if the spirit appears visibly, I will speak to it.*

He was preparing to descend the staircase, when he heard several knocks at the door by which he first entered the room; and, stepping backward, the door was clapped to with great violence. Again fear attacked him, but he resisted it, and boldly cried out— Who is there?—A voice at the outer door answered,—It's I— Joseph, your friend!—What do you want, said Edmund?—I have brought you some wood to make a fire, said Joseph.—I thank you kindly, said Edmund; but my lamp is gone out; I will try to find the door, however. After some trouble he found, and opened it; and was not sorry to see his friend Joseph with a light in one hand, a flaggon of beer in the other, and a faggot upon his shoulder. I come, said the good old man, to bring you something to keep up your spirits; the evening is cold; I know this room wants airing; and beside that, my Master, I think your present undertaking requires a little assistance.

My good friend, said Edmund, I never shall be able to deserve or requite your kindness to me.—My dear Sir, you always deserved more than I could do for you; and I think I shall yet live to see you defeat the designs of your enemies, and acknowledge the services of your friends.—Alas, said Edmund, I see little prospect of that!—I see, said Joseph, something that persuades me you are designed for great things; and I perceive that things are working about to some great end: Have courage, my Master, my heart beats strangely high upon your account!—You make me smile, said Edmund.—I am glad to see it, Sir; may you smile all the rest of your life.—I thank your honest affection, returned Edmund, though it is too partial to me. You had better go to bed, however; if it is known that you visit me here, it will be bad for us both.—So I will presently; but, please God, I will come here again to-morrow night when all the family are a-bed; and I will tell you some things that you never yet heard.—But pray tell me, said Edmund, where does that door lead to?—Upon a passage that ends in a staircase that leads to the lower rooms; and there is likewise a door out of that passage into the dining-room.—And what rooms are there below stairs, said Edmund?—The same as above, replied he.—Very well; then I wish you a good night, we will talk further to-morrow.—Aye, to-morrow night; and in this place, my dear Master.—Why do you call me your Master? I never was, nor ever can be, your Master.—God only knows that, said the good old man; good night, and Heaven bless you!—good night, my worthy friend!

Joseph withdrew, and Edmund returned to the other door, and attempted several times to open it in vain; his hands were benumbed and tired; at length he gave over. He made a fire in the chimney, placed the lamp on a table, and opened one of the window-shutters to admit the day-light; he then recommended himself to the divine protection, and threw himself upon the bed; he presently fell asleep, and continued in that state, till the sun saluted him with his orient beams through the window he had opened.

As soon as he was perfectly awake he strove to recollect his dreams. He thought that he heard people coming up the staircase that he had a glimpse of; that the door opened, and there entered a Warrior, leading a Lady by the hand, who was young and beautiful, but pale and wan: The Man was dressed in complete armour, and his helmet down. They approached the bed; they undrew the curtains. He thought the Man said,—Is this our child? The woman replied,—It is; and the hour approaches that he shall be known for such. They then separated, and one stood on each side of the bed; their hands met over his head, and they gave him a solemn benediction. He strove to rise and pay them his respects, but they forbad him; and the Lady said,—Sleep in peace, oh my Edmund! for those who are the true possessors of this apartment are employed in thy preservation: Sleep on, sweet hope of a house that is thought past hope!—Upon this they withdrew, and went out at the same door by which they entered, and he heard them descend the stairs.—After this, he followed a funeral as chief mourner; he saw the whole procession, and heard the ceremonies performed. He was snatched away from this mournful scene to one of a contrary kind, a stately feast, at which he presided; and he heard himself congratulated as a husband and a father: His friend William sat by his side; and his happiness was complete.

Every succeeding idea was happiness without allay; and his mind was not idle a moment till the morning sun awakened him. He perfectly remembered his dreams, and meditated on what all these things should portend. Am I then, said he, not Edmund Twyford, but somebody of consequence in whose fate so many people are interested? Vain thought, that must have arisen from the partial suggestion of my two friends, Mr. William and old Joseph!

He lay thus reflecting, when a servant knocked at his door, and told him it was past six o'clock, and that the Baron expected him to breakfast in an hour. He rose immediately; paid his tribute of thanks to Heaven for its protection, and went from his chamber in high health and spirits.

He walked in the garden till the hour of breakfast, and then attended the Baron. Good morrow, Edmund! said he; how have you rested in your new apartment? Extremely well my Lord, answered he.—I am glad to hear it, said the Baron; but I did not know your accommodations were so bad, as Joseph tells me they are.—'Tis of no consequence, said Edmund; if they were much worse I could dispense with them for three nights.—Very well, said the Baron; you are a brave lad: I am satisfied with you, and will excuse the other two nights.—But, my Lord, I will not be excused; no one shall have reason to suspect my courage: I am determined to go through the remaining nights upon many accounts.—That shall be as you please, said my Lord. I think of you as you deserve; so well, that I shall ask your advice by and by in some affairs of consequence.—My life and services are yours, my Lord; command them freely.—Let Oswald be called in, said my Lord; he shall be one of our consultation. He came; the servants were dismissed; and the Baron spoke as follows. Edmund, when first I took you into my family, it was at the request of my sons and kinsmen; I bear witness to your good behaviour, you have not deserved to lose their esteem; but, nevertheless, I have observed for some years past, that all but my son William have set their faces against you: I see their meanness, and I perceive their motives: But they are, and must be, my relations; and I would rather govern them by love, than fear. I love and esteem your virtues: I cannot give you up to gratify their humours. My son William has lost the affections of the rest, for that he bears to you; but he has increased my regard for him: I think myself bound in honour to him and you, to provide for you; I cannot do it, as I wished, under my own roof. If you stay here I see nothing but confusion in my family; yet I cannot put you out of it disgracefully. I want to think of some way to prefer you, that you may leave this house with honour; and I desire both of you to give me your advice in this matter. If Edmund will tell me in what way I can employ him to his own honour and my advantage, I am ready to do it; let him propose it, and Oswald shall moderate between us.

Here he stopped; and Edmund, whose sighs almost choaked him, threw himself at the Baron's feet, and wet his hand with his tears. Oh, my noble generous benefactor! do you condescend to consult such a one as me upon the state of your family? does your most amiable and beloved son incur the ill will of his brothers and kinsmen for my sake? What am I, that I should disturb the peace of this noble family? Oh, my Lord, send me away directly! I should be unworthy to live if I did not earnestly endeavour to restore your happiness. You have given me a noble education, and I trust I shall not disgrace it. If you will recommend me, and give me a character, I fear not to make my own fortune. The Baron wiped his eyes; I wish to do this my child, but in what way?—My Lord, said Edmund, I will open my heart to you. I have served with credit in the army, and I should prefer a soldier's life.—You please me well, said the Baron: I will send you to France, and give you a recommendation to the Regent; he knows you personally, and will prefer you, for my sake, and for your own merit.—My Lord, you overwhelm me with your goodness! I am but your creature, and my life shall be devoted to your service.—But, said the Baron, how to dispose of you till the spring?—That, said Oswald, may be thought of at leisure; I am glad that you have resolved, and I congratulate you both. The Baron put an end to the conversation by desiring Edmund to go with him into the Manage* to see his horses. He ordered Oswald to acquaint his son William with all that had passed, and to try to persuade the young men to meet Edmund and William at dinner.

The Baron took Edmund with him into his Manage to see some horses he had lately purchased; while they were examining the beauties and defects of these noble and useful animals, Edmund declared that he preferred Caradoc,* a horse he had broke himself, to any other in my Lord's stables. Then, said the Baron, I will give him to you; and you shall go upon him to seek your fortune. He made new acknowledgments for this gift, and declared he would prize it highly for the giver's sake. But I shall not part with you yet, said my Lord; I will first carry all my points with these saucy* boys, and oblige them to do you justice. — You have already done that, said Edmund; and I will not suffer any of your Lordship's blood to undergo any farther humiliation upon my account. I think, with humble submission to your better judgment, the sooner I go hence the better.

While they were speaking, Oswald came to them, and said, that the young men had absolutely refused to dine at the table, if Edmund was present. 'Tis well, said the Baron; I shall find a way to punish their contumacy hereafter: I will make them know that I am the master here. Edmund and you, Oswald, shall spend the day in my apartment above stairs. William shall dine with me alone; and I will acquaint him with our determination: My son Robert, and his cabal, shall be prisoners in the great parlour. Edmund shall, according to his own desire, spend this and the following night in the haunted apartment; and this for his sake and my own; for if I should now contradict my former orders, it would subject us both to their impertinent reflections.

He then took Oswald aside, and charged him not to let Edmund go out of his sight; for if he should come in the way of those implacable enemies, he trembled for the consequences. He then walked back to the stables, and the two friends returned into the house.

They had a long conversation on various subjects; in the course of it, Edmund acquainted Oswald with all that had passed between him and Joseph the preceding night, the curiosity he had raised in him, and his promise to gratify it the night following. I wish, said Oswald, you would permit me to be one of your party.—How can that be, said Edmund? we shall be watched perhaps; and, if discovered, what excuse can you make for coming there? Beside, if it were known, I shall be branded with the imputation of cowardice, and though I have borne much, I will not promise to bear that patiently.—Never fear, replied Oswald, I will speak to Joseph about it, and after prayers are over and the family gone to bed, I will steal away from my own chamber and come to you. I am strongly interested in your affairs; and I cannot be easy unless you will receive me into your company: I will bind myself to secrecy in any manner you shall enjoin.—Your word is sufficient, said Edmund; I have as much reason to trust you, Father, as any man living; I should be ungrateful to refuse you any thing in my power to grant: But suppose the apartment should really be haunted, would you have resolution enough to pursue the adventure to a discovery?—I hope so, said Oswald: But have you any reason to believe it is?—I have, said Edmund; but I have not opened my lips upon this subject to any creature but yourself. This night I purpose, if Heaven permit, to go all over the rooms; and though I had formed this design, I will confess that your company will strengthen my resolution. I will have no reserves to you in any respect; but I must put a seal upon your lips. Oswald swore secrecy till he should be permitted to disclose the mysteries of that apartment; and both of them waited, in solemn expectation, the event of the approaching night.

In the afternoon Mr. William was allowed to visit his friend: An affecting interview passed between them: He lamented the necessity of Edmund's departure; and they took a solemn leave of each other, as if they foreboded it would be long e'er they should meet again.

About the same hour as the preceding evening, Joseph came to conduct Edmund to his apartment. You will find better accommodations than you had last night, said he, and all by my Lord's own order.—I every hour receive some new proof of his goodness, said Edmund. When they arrived, he found a good fire in the chamber, and a table covered with cold meats, and a flaggon of strong beer. Sit down and get your supper, my dear Master, said Joseph: I must attend my Lord; but as soon as the family are gone to bed I will visit you again.—Do so, said Edmund; but first, see Father Oswald; he has something to say to you: You may trust him, for I have no reserves to him.—Well, Sir, I will see him if you desire it; and I will come to you as soon as possible. So saying, he went his way; and Edmund sat down to supper.

After a moderate refreshment he kneeled down, and prayed with the greatest fervency; he resigned himself to the disposal of Heaven: I am nothing, said he, I desire to be nothing but what thou, O Lord, pleasest to make me: If it is thy will that I should return to my former obscurity, be it obeyed with chearfulness! and, if thou art pleased to exalt me, I will look up to thee as the only fountain of honour and dignity. While he prayed, he felt an enlargement of heart beyond what he had ever experienced before; all idle fears were dispersed, and his heart glowed with divine love and affiance: He seemed raised above the world and all its pursuits. He continued wrapt up in mental devotion, till a knocking at the door obliged him to rise, and let in his two friends, who came without shoes, and on tiptoe, to visit him.

Save you, my son! said the friar; you look chearful and happy.—I am so, Father, said Edmund; I have resigned myself to the disposal of Heaven, and I find my heart strengthened above what I can express.—Heaven be praised! said Oswald: I believe you are designed for great things, my son.—What! do you too encourage my ambition? says Edmund; strange concurrence of circumstances! Sit down, my friends; and do you, my good Joseph, tell me the particulars you promised last night. They drew their chairs round the fire, and Joseph began as follows.

You have heard of the untimely death of the late Lord Lovel, my noble and worthy Master; perhaps you may have also heard that, from that time, this apartment was haunted. What passed the other day, when my Lord questioned you both on this head, brought all the circumstances fresh into my mind. You then said, there were suspicions that he came not fairly to his end. I trust you both, and will speak what I know of it. There was a person suspected of this murder; and whom do you think it was?—You must speak out, said Oswald.—Why then, said Joseph, it was the present Lord Lovel.—You speak my thoughts, said Oswald; but proceed to the proofs.—I will, said Joseph. From the time that my Lord's death was reported, there were strange whisperings and consultations between the new Lord and some of the servants; there was a deal of private business carried on in this apartment: Soon after, they gave out that my poor Lady was distracted; but she threw out strong expressions that favoured nothing of madness: She said, that the ghost of her departed Lord had appeared to her, and revealed the circumstances of this murder. None of the servants, but one, were permitted to see her. At this very time Sir Walter, the new Lord, had the cruelty to offer love to her; he urged her to marry him; and one of her women overheard her say, she would sooner die than give her hand to the man who caused the death of her Lord: Soon after this, we were told my Lady was dead. The Lord Lovel made a publick and sumptuous funeral for her.—That is true, said Oswald; for I was a novice, and assisted at it.

Well, says Joseph, now comes my part of the story. As I was coming home from the burial, I overtook Roger our plowman. Said he, What think you of this burying? What should I think, said I, but that we have lost the best Master and Lady that we shall ever know? God he knows, quoth Roger, whether they be living or dead; but if ever I saw my Lady in my life, I saw her alive the night they say she died. I tried to convince him that he was mistaken; but he offered to take his oath, that the very night they said she died, he saw her come out at the garden gate into the fields; that she often stopped, like a person in pain, and then went forward again until he lost sight of her. Now it is certain that her time was out, and she expected to lay down every day: and they did not pretend that she died in childbed. I thought upon what I heard, but nothing I said. Roger told the same story to another servant; so he was called to an account, the story was hushed up, and the foolish fellow said, he was verily persuaded it was her ghost that he saw. Now you must take notice that from this time, they began to talk about that this apartment was troubled: and not only this, but at last the new Lord could not sleep in quiet in his own room; and this induced him to sell the castle to his brother-in-law, and get out of this country as fast as possible. He took most of the servants away with him, and Roger among the rest. As for me, they thought I knew nothing, and so they left me behind; but I was neither blind nor deaf, though I could hear, and see, and say nothing.

This is a dark story, said Oswald.—It is so, said Edmund; but why should Joseph seem to think it concerns me in particular?— Ah, dear Sir! said Joseph, I must tell you, though I never uttered it to mortal man before; the striking resemblance this young man bears to my dear Lord, the strange dislike his reputed father took to him, his gentle manners, his generous heart, his noble qualities so uncommon in those of his birth and breeding, the sound of his voice—You may smile at the strength of my fancy, but I cannot put it out of my mind but that he is my own Master's son.

At these words Edmund changed colour and trembled; he clapped his hand upon his breast, and looked up to Heaven in silence; his dream recurred to his memory, and struck upon his heart. He related it to his attentive auditors. The ways of providence are wonderful, said Oswald! If this be so, Heaven in its own time will make it appear.

Here a silence of several minutes ensued; when, suddenly, they were awakened from their reverie by a violent noise in the rooms underneath them. It seemed like the clashing of arms, and something seemed to fall down with violence.

They started, and Edmund rose up with a look full of resolution and intrepidity.—I am called! said he; I obey the call! He took up a lamp, and went to the door that he had opened the night before. Oswald followed with his rosary in his hand, and Joseph last with trembling steps. The door opened with ease, and they descended the stairs in profound silence.

The lower rooms answered exactly to those above; there were two parlours and a large closet. They saw nothing remarkable in these rooms, except two pictures that were turned with their faces to the wall. Joseph took the courage to turn them: These, said he, are the portraits of my late Lord and Lady. Father, look at this face, do you know who is like it?—I should think, said Oswald, it was done for Edmund!—I am, said Edmund, struck with the resemblance myself: But let us go on, I feel myself inspired with unusual courage.—Let us open the closet door.—Oswald stopped him short; Take heed, said he, lest the wind of the door put out the lamp. I will open this door. He attempted it without success; Joseph did the same, but to no purpose: Edmund gave the lamp to Joseph, he approached the door, tried the key, and it gave way to his hand in a moment. This adventure belongs, said he, to me only, that is plain; bring the lamp forward. Oswald repeated the paternoster,* in which they all joined, and then entered the closet.

The first thing that presented itself to their view was a compleat suit of armour that seemed to have fallen down on an heap. Behold! said Edmund; this made the noise we heard above. They took it up, and examined it piece by piece; the inside of the breast-plate was stained with blood. See here! said Edmund; what think you of this?—'Tis my Lord's armour, said Joseph; I know it well: Here has been bloody work in this closet!—Going forward he stumbled over something; it was a ring with the arms of Lovel engraved upon it. This is my Lord's ring, said Joseph; I have seen him wear it: I give it to you, Sir, as the right owner; and most religiously do I believe you his son. Heaven only knows that, said Edmund; and, if it permits, I will know who was my father before I am a day older. While he was speaking he shifted his ground, and perceived that the boards rose up on the other side of the closet; upon farther examination they found that the whole floor was loose, and a table that stood over them concealed the circumstance from a casual observer. I perceive, said Oswald, that some great discovery is at hand.—God defend us! said Edmund, but I verily believe that the person that owned this armour lies buried under us. Upon this, a dismal hollow groan was heard as if from underneath. A solemn silence ensued, and marks of fear were visible upon all three; the groan was thrice heard: Oswald made signs for them to kneel, and he prayed audibly, that Heaven would direct them how to act; he also prayed for the soul of the departed, that it might rest in peace. After this he arose; but Edmund continued kneeling: He vowed solemnly to devote himself to the discovery of this secret, and the avenging the death of the person there buried. He then rose up. It would be to no purpose, said he, for us to examine further now, when I am properly authorised I will have this place opened: I trust that time is not far off.—I believe it, said Oswald; you are designed by Heaven to be its instrument in bringing this deed of darkness to light. We are your creatures, only tell us what you would have us do, and we are ready to obey your commands.—I only demand your silence, said Edmund, till I call for your evidence; and then, you must speak all you know, and all you suspect.—Oh, said Joseph, that I may but live to see that day, and I shall have lived long enough!—Come, said Edmund, let us return up stairs, and we will consult further how I shall proceed: So saying, he went out of the closet, and they followed him. He locked the door, and took the key out: I will keep this, said he, till I have power to use it to purpose, lest any one should presume to pry into the secret of this closet: I will always carry it about me, to remind me of what I have undertaken.

Upon this, they returned up stairs into the bed-chamber; all was still, and they heard nothing more to disturb them. How, said Edmund, is it possible that I should be the son of Lord Lovel? for, however circumstances have seemed to encourage such a notion, what reason have I to believe it?—I am strangely puzzled about it, said Oswald. It seems unlikely that so good a man as Lord Lovel should corrupt the wife of a peasant, his vassal; and, especially, being so lately married to a Lady with whom he was passionately in love.—Hold there! said Joseph; my Lord was incapable of such an action: If Master Edmund is the son of my Lord, he is also the son of my Lady.—How can that be, said Edmund?—I don't know how, said Joseph; but there is a person who can tell if she will: I mean Margery Twyford, who calls herself your mother.—You meet my thoughts, said Edmund; I had resolved, before you spoke, to visit her, and to interrogate her on the subject: I will ask my Lord's permission to go this very day.—That is right, said Oswald; but be cautious and prudent in your enquiries.—If you, said Edmund, would bear me company I should do better; she might think herself obliged to answer your questions; and, being less interested in the event, you would be more discreet in your interrogations. That I will most readily, said he; and I will ask my Lord's permission for us both.—This point is well determined, said Joseph; I am impatient for the result; and I believe my feet will carry me to meet you whether I consent or not.—I am as impatient as you, said Oswald; but let us be silent as the grave, and let not a word or look indicate any thing knowing or mysterious.

The day-light began to dawn upon their conference; and Edmund, observing it, begged his friends to withdraw in silence. They did so, and left Edmund to his own recollections. His thoughts were too much employed for sleep to approach him; he threw himself upon the bed, and lay meditating how he should proceed; a thousand schemes offered themselves and were rejected: But he resolved, at all events, to leave Baron Fitz-Owen's family the first opportunity that presented itself.

He was summoned, as before, to attend my Lord at breakfast; during which, he was silent, absent, and reserved. My Lord observed it, and rallied him; enquiring how he had spent the night?—In reflecting upon my situation, my Lord; and in laying plans for my future conduct. Oswald took the hint, and asked permission to visit Edmund's mother in his company, and acquaint her with his intentions of leaving the country soon. He consented freely; but seemed unresolved about Edmund's departure.

They set out directly, and Edmund went hastily to old Twyford's cottage, declaring that every field seemed a mile to him. Restrain your warmth my son, said Oswald; compose your mind, and recover your breath, before you enter upon a business of such consequence. Margery met them at the door, and asked Edmund, what wind blew him thither? Is it so very surprising, said he, that I should visit my parents?—Yes it is, said she, considering the treatment you have met with from us; but since Andrew is not in the house I may say I am glad to see you: Lord bless you, what a fine youth you be grown! 'Tis a long time since I saw you; but that is not my fault: Many a cross word, and many a blow have I had on your account; but I may now venture to embrace my dear child.—Edmund came forward and embraced her fervently; the starting tears, on both sides, evinced their affection. And why, said he, should my father forbid you to embrace your child? what have I ever done to deserve his hatred?—Nothing, my dear boy! you were always good and tender hearted, and deserved the love of every body.—It is not common, said Edmund, for a parent to hate his first born son without his having deserved it.—That is true, said Oswald; it is uncommon, it is unnatural; nay, I am of opinion it is almost impossible. I am so convinced of this truth, that I believe the man who thus hates and abuses Edmund, cannot be his father. In saying this, he observed her countenance attentively; she changed colour apparently. Come, said he, let us sit down; and do you Margery answer to what I have said: Blessed Virgin! said Margery, what does your Reverence mean? what do you suspect?—I suspect, said he, that Edmund is not the son of Andrew your husband.—Lord bless me, said she, what is it you do suspect?—Do not evade my question, woman! I am come here by authority to examine you upon this point. The woman trembled every joint: Would to Heaven! said she, that Andrew was at home!—It is much better as it is, said Oswald: You are the person we are to examine.—Oh, Father, said she, do you think that I— that I—that I am to blame in this matter? what have I done?—Do you, Sir, said he, ask your own questions. Upon this, Edmund threw himself at her feet, and embraced her knees. Oh my mother, said he, for as such my heart owns you, tell me for the love of Heaven! tell me who was my father?—Gracious Heaven? said she, what will become of me?—Woman! said Oswald, confess the truth or you shall be compelled to do it: By whom had you this youth?—Who, I! said she; I had him! No, Father, I am not guilty of the black crime of adultery; God he knows my innocence: I am not worthy to be the mother of such a sweet youth as that is.—You are not his mother then, nor Andrew his father?— Oh, what shall I do! said Margery; Andrew will be the death of me!—No, he shall not, said Edmund; you shall be protected and rewarded for the discovery.—Goody,* said Oswald, confess the whole truth, and I will protect you from harm and from blame; you may be the means of making Edmund's fortune, in which case he will certainly provide for you; on the other hand, by an obstinate silence you will deprive yourself of all advantages you might receive from the discovery; and, beside, you will soon be examined in a different manner, and be obliged to confess all you know, and nobody will thank you for it.—Ah, said she, but Andrew beat me the last time I spoke to Edmund; and told me he would break every bone in my skin if ever I spoke to him again.— He knows it then, said Oswald?—He know it! Lord help you, it was all his own doing.—Tell us then, said Oswald, for Andrew shall never know it, till it is out of his power to punish you.— 'Tis a long story, said she, and cannot be told in a few words.— It will never be told at this rate, said he; sit down and begin it instantly.—My fate depends upon your words, said Edmund; my soul is impatient of the suspence! If ever you loved me and cherished me, shew it now, and tell while I have breath to ask it.

He sat in extreme agitation of mind; his words and actions were equally expressive of his inward emotions. I will, said she; but I must try to recollect all the circumstances. You must know, young man, that you are just one and twenty years of age.—On what day was he born, said Oswald?—The day before yesterday, said she, the 21st of September.—A remarkable æra, said he.— 'Tis so indeed, said Edmund: Oh, that night! that apartment!— Be silent, said Oswald; and do you, Margery, begin your story.

I will, said she. Just one and twenty years ago, on that very day, I lost my first born son: I got a hurt by over-reaching myself when I was near my time, and so the poor child died. And so, as I was sitting all alone, and very melancholy, Andrew came home from work: See Margery, said he, I have brought you a child instead of that you have lost. So he gave me a bundle, as I thought; but sure enough it was a child; a poor helpless babe just born, and only rolled up in a fine handkerchief, and over that a rich velvet cloak, trimmed with gold lace. And where did you find this? said I.—Upon the foot bridge, says he, just below the clay field. This child, said he, belongs to some great folk, and perhaps it may be enquired after one day, and may make our fortunes; take care of it, said he, and bring it up as if it was your own. The poor infant was cold, and it cried, and looked up at me so pitifully, that

I loved it; beside my milk was troublesome to me, and I was glad to be eased of it, so I gave it the breast, and from that hour I loved the child as if it were my own, and so I do still if I dared to own it.—And this is all you know of Edmund's birth? said Oswald.—No, not all, said Margery; but pray look out and see whether Andrew is coming, for I am all over in a twitter.—He is not, said Oswald; go on I beseech you!—This happened, said she, as I told you, on the 21st. On the morrow my Andrew went out early to work, along with one Robin Rouse, our neighbour; they had not been gone above an hour when they both came back seemingly very much frightened: Says Andrew, go you Robin and borrow a pick-axe at neighbour Styles's. What is the matter now, said I?—Matter enough, quoth Andrew! we may come to be hanged perhaps, as many an innocent man has before us. Tell me what is the matter? said I. I will, said he; but if ever you open your mouth about it, woe be to you! I never will, said I: But he made me swear by all the blessed Saints in the Calendar; and then he told me, that as Robin and he were going over the foot bridge, where he found the child the evening before, they saw something floating upon the water; so they followed it, till it stuck against a stake, and found it to be the dead body of a woman: As sure as you are alive Madge, said he, this was the mother of the child I brought home.—Merciful God! said Edmund; am I the child of that hapless mother?—Be composed, said Oswald: Proceed, good woman, the time is precious.—And so, continued she, Andrew told me they dragged the body out of the river, and it was richly dressed, and must be somebody of consequence. I suppose, said he, when the poor Lady had taken care of her child, she went to find some help; and, the night being dark, her foot slipped, and she fell into the river and was drowned.

Lord have mercy! said Robin, what shall we do with the dead body? we may be taken up for the murder; what had we to do to meddle with it? Ay, but, says Andrew, we must have something to do with it now; and our wisest way is to bury it. Robin was sadly frightened, but at last they agreed to carry it into the wood and bury it there; so they came home for a pick-axe and shovel. Well, said I, Andrew, but will you bury all the rich clothes you speak of? Why, said he, it would be both a sin and a shame to strip the dead. So it would, said I; but I will give you a sheet to wrap the body in, and you may take off her upper garments, and any thing of value; but do not strip her to the skin for any thing. Well said, wench! said he; I will do as you say. So I fetched a sheet, and by that time Robin was come back, and away they went together.

They did not come back again till noon, and then they sat down and ate a morsel together. Says Andrew, Now we may sit down and eat in peace. Ay, says Robin, and sleep in peace too, for we have done no harm. No, to be sure, said I; but yet I am much concerned that the poor Lady had not Christian burial. Never trouble thyself about that, said Andrew; we have done the best we could for her: But let us see what we have got in our bags, we must divide them. So they opened their bags, and took out a fine gown and a pair of rich shoes; but besides these, there was a fine necklace with a golden locket, and a pair of ear-rings. Says Andrew, and winked at me, I will have these, and you may take the rest. Robin said he was satisfied, and so he went his way. When he was gone, Here you fool, says Andrew, take these, and keep them as safe as the bud of your eye: If ever young Master is found, these will make our fortune.—And have you them now? said Oswald.—Yes, that I have, answered she; Andrew would have sold them long ago, but I always put him off it.—Heaven be praised! said Edmund.—Hush, said Oswald, let us not lose time; proceed, Goody!—Nay, said Margery, I have not much more to say. We looked every day to hear some enquiries after the child, but nothing passed, nobody was missing.—Did nobody of note die about that time? said Oswald.—Why yes, said Margery, the widow Lady Lovel died that same week: By the same token, Andrew went to the funeral and brought home a 'scutcheon, which I keep unto this day.—Very well; go on.—My husband behaved well enough to the boy till such time as he had two or three children of his own; and then he began to grumble, and say, it was hard to maintain other folks children, when he found it hard enough to keep his own: I loved the boy quite as well as my own; often and often have I pacified Andrew, and made him to hope that he should one day or other be paid for his trouble; but at last he grew out of patience, and gave over all hopes of that kind.

As Edmund grew up, he grew sickly and tender, and could not bear hard labour; and that was another reason why my husband could not bear with him. If, quoth he, the boy could earn his living I did not care; but I must bear all the expence. There came an old pilgrim into our parts, he was a scholar, and had been a soldier, and he taught Edmund to read; then he told him histories of wars, and Knights, and Lords, and great men; and Edmund took such delight in hearing him, that he would not take to any thing else.

To be sure Edwin was a pleasant companion, he would tell old stories, and sing old songs, that one could have sat all night to hear him; but, as I was a saying, Edmund grew more and more fond of reading and less of work; however, he would run of errands and do many handy turns for the neighbours; and he was so courteous a lad that people took notice of him. Andrew once catched him alone reading, and then told him, that if he did not find some way to earn his bread, he would turn him out of doors in a very short time; and so he would have done sure enough, if my Lord Fitz-Owen had not taken him into his service just in the nick.

Very well, Goody, said Oswald; you have told your story very well; I am glad for Edmund's sake, that you can do it so properly: But now, can you keep a secret?—Why an't please your Reverence, I think I have showed you that I can.—But can you keep it from your husband? Aye, said she, surely I can; for I dare not tell it him.—That is a good security, said he; but I must have a better: You must swear upon this book not to disclose any thing that has passed between us three, till we desire you to do it. Be assured you will soon be called upon for this purpose. Edmund's birth is near the discovery: He is the son of parents of high degree; and it will be in his power to make your fortune when he takes possession of his own.

Holy Virgin! what is it you tell me? How you rejoice me to hear, that what I have so long prayed for will come to pass!—She took the oath required, saying after Oswald.—Now, said he, go and fetch the tokens you have mentioned.

When she was gone, Edmund's passions, long suppressed, broke out in tears and exclamations; he kneeled down, and, with his hands clasped together, returned thanks to Heaven for the discovery. Oswald begged him to be composed, lest Margery should perceive his agitation, and misconstrue the cause. She soon returned with the necklace and ear-rings: They were pearls of great value; and the necklace had a locket, on which the cypher of Lovel was engraved. This, said Oswald, is indeed a proof of consequence: Keep it, Sir, for it belongs to you.—Must he take it away? said she.—Certainly, returned Oswald; we can do nothing without it: But if Andrew should ask for it, you must put him off for the present, and hereafter he will find his account in it. Margery consented reluctantly to part with the jewels; and, after some further conversation, they took leave of her. Edmund embraced her affectionately. I thank you with my whole heart, said he, for all your goodness to me! Though I confess, I never felt much regard for your husband, yet for you I had always the tender affection of a son. You will, I trust, give your evidence in my behalf when called upon; and I hope it will one day be in my power to reward your kindness: In that case, I will own you as my foster-mother, and you shall always be treated as such.— Margery wept. The Lord grant it! said she; and I pray him to have you in his holy keeping. Farewell, my dear child!—Oswald desired them to separate for fear of intrusion; and they returned to the Castle. Margery stood at the door of her cottage, looking every way to see if the coast was clear.

Now, Sir, said Oswald, I congratulate you as the son of Lord and Lady Lovel! the proofs are strong and indisputable. To us they are so, said Edmund; but how shall we make them so to others? and what are we to think of the funeral of Lady Lovel?— As of a fiction, said Oswald; the work of the present Lord, to secure his title and fortune.—And what means can we use to dispossess him? said Edmund: He is not a man for a poor youth like me to contend with.—Doubt not, said Oswald, but Heaven, who has evidently conducted you by the hand thus far, will com-

pleat its own work; for my part, I can only wonder and adore!—
Give me your advice then, said Edmund; for Heaven assists us by
natural means.

It seems to me, said Oswald, that your first step must be to
make a friend of some great man, of consequence enough to
espouse your cause, and to get this affair examined into by authority. Edmund started, and crossed himself; he suddenly
exclaimed—A friend! Yes; I have a friend! a powerful one too; one
sent by Heaven to be my protector, but whom I have too long neglected.—Who can that be? said Oswald.—Who should it be, said
Edmund, but that good Sir Philip Harclay, the chosen friend of
him, whom I shall from henceforward call my father.—'Tis true
indeed, said Oswald; and this is a fresh proof of what I before
observed, that Heaven assists you, and will compleat its own
work.—I think so myself, said Edmund, and rely upon its direction. I have already determined on my future conduct, which I
will communicate to you. My first step shall be to leave the Castle; my Lord has this day given me a horse, upon which I purpose
to set out this very night, without the knowledge of any of the
family. I will go to Sir Philip Harclay; I will throw myself at his
feet, relate my strange story, and implore his protection: With
him I will consult on the most proper way of bringing this murderer to public justice; and I will be guided by his advice and
direction in every thing.—Nothing can be better, said Oswald,
than what you propose; but give me leave to offer an addition to
your scheme. You shall set off in the dead of night as you intend;
Joseph and I will favour your departure in such a manner as to
throw a mystery over the circumstances of it: Your disappearing
at such a time from the haunted apartment, will terrify and con-
found all the family; they will puzzle themselves in vain to
account for it, and they will be afraid to pry into the secrets of
that place.

You say well, and I approve your addition, replied Edmund.
Suppose, likewise, there was a letter written in a mysterious manner, and dropt in my Lord's way, or sent to him afterwards; it
would forward our design, and frighten them away from
that apartment.—That shall be my care, said Oswald; and I will

warrant you that they will not find themselves disposed to inhabit it presently.—But how shall I leave my dear friend Mr. William, without a word of notice of this separation?—I have thought of that too, said Oswald; and I will so manage, as to acquaint him with it in such a manner as he shall think out of the common course of things, and which shall make him wonder and be silent.—How will you do that, said Edmund?—I will tell you hereafter, said Oswald; for here comes old Joseph to meet us.

He came, indeed, as fast as his age would permit him. As soon as he was within hearing, he asked them what news? They related all that had passed at Twyford's cottage; he heard them with the greatest eagerness of attention, and as soon as they came to the great event—I knew it! I knew it! exclaimed Joseph; I was sure it would prove so! Thank God for it! But I will be the first to acknowledge my young Lord, and I will live and die his faithful servant! Here Joseph attempted to kneel to him, but Edmund prevented him with a warm embrace: My friend, my dear friend! said he, I cannot suffer a man of your age to kneel to me; are you not one of my best and truest friends? I will ever remember your disinterested affection for me; and if Heaven restores me to my rights, it shall be one of my first cares to render your old age easy and happy. Joseph wept over him, and it was some time before he could utter a word.

Oswald gave them both time to recover their emotion, by acquainting Joseph with Edmund's scheme for his departure. Joseph wiped his eyes and spoke. I have thought, said he, of something that will be both agreeable and useful to my dear Master. John Wyatt, Sir Philip Harclay's servant, is now upon a visit at his father's; I have heard that he goes home soon; now he would be both a guide, and companion, on the way.—That is, indeed, a happy circumstance, said Edmund; but how shall we know certainly the time of his departure?—Why, Sir, I will go to him, and enquire; and bring you word directly.—Do so, said Edmund, and you will oblige me greatly.—But, Sir, said Oswald, I think it will be best not to let John Wyatt know who is to be his companion; only let Joseph tell him that a gentleman is going to visit his Master: And, if possible, prevail upon him to set out this night.—Do so, my good friend, said Edmund; and tell him, further, that this person has business of great consequence to communicate to his Master, and cannot delay his journey on any account.—I will do this you may depend, said Joseph, and acquaint you with my success as soon as possible; but, Sir, you must not go without a guide, at any rate.—I trust I shall not, said Edmund, though I go alone; he that has received such a call as I have, can want no other, nor fear any danger.

They conversed on these points till they drew near the castle, when Joseph left them to go on his errand, and Edmund attended his Lord at dinner. The Baron observed that he was silent and reserved; the conversation languished on both sides. As soon as dinner was ended, Edmund asked permission to go up into his own apartment; where he packed up some necessaries, and made a hasty preparation for his departure.

Afterwards he walked into the garden, revolving in his mind the peculiarity of his situation, and the uncertainty of his future prospects; lost in thought, he walked to and fro in a covered walk, with his arms crost and his eyes cast down, without perceiving that he was observed by two females who stood at a distance watching his motions: It was the Lady Emma, and her attendant, who were thus engaged. At length, he lifted up his eyes and saw them: he stood still, and was irresolute whether to advance or retire: They approached him; and, as they drew near, fair Emma spoke. You have been so wrapt in meditation, Edmund, that I am apprehensive of some new vexation that I am yet a stranger to: Would it were in my power to lessen those you have already! But tell me if I guess truly?—He stood still irresolute, he answered with hesitation. Oh, Lady—I am—I am grieved, I am concerned, to be the cause of so much confusion in this noble family, to which I am so much indebted: I see no way to lessen these evils but to remove the cause of them.—Meaning yourself? said she.—Certainly, Madam; and I was meditating on my departure.—But, said she, by your departure you will not remove the cause.—How so, Madam?—Because you are not the cause, but those you will leave behind you.—Lady Emma!—How can you affect this ignorance, Edmund? You know well enough it is that odious

Wenlock, your enemy and my aversion, that has caused all this mischief among us, and will much more if he is not removed.—This, Madam, is a subject that it becomes me to be silent upon: Mr. Wenlock is your kinsman; he is not my friend; and for that reason I ought not to speak against him, nor you to hear it from me: If he has used me ill, I am recompenced by the generous treatment of my Lord your father, who is all that is great and good; he has allowed me to justify myself to him, and he has restored me to his good opinion, which I prize among the best gifts of heaven: Your amiable brother William thinks well of me, and his esteem is infinitely dear to me; and you, excellent Lady, permit me to hope that you honour me with your good opinion: Are not these ample amends for the ill-will Mr. Wenlock bears me?—My opinion of you, Edmund, said she, is fixed and settled: It is not founded upon events of yesterday, but upon long knowledge and experience; upon your whole conduct and character.—You honour me, Lady! Continue to think well of me, it will excite me to deserve it. When I am far distant from this place, the remembrance of your goodness will be a cordial to my heart.—But why will you leave us, Edmund? stay and defeat the designs of your enemy; you shall have my wishes and assistance.—Pardon me, Madam, that is among the things I cannot do, even if it were in my power, which it is not. Mr. Wenlock loves you, Lady, and if he is so unhappy as to be your aversion, that is a punishment severe enough. For the rest, I may be unfortunate by the wickedness of others, but if I am unworthy it must be by my own fault.—So then you think it is an unworthy action to oppose Mr. Wenlock! Very well, Sir: Then I suppose you wish him success; you wish that I may be married to him?—I, Madam? said Edmund, confused; what am I that I should give my opinion on an affair of so much consequence? You distress me by the question. May you be happy! may you enjoy your own wishes! He sighed, he turned away. She called him back; he trembled, and kept silence.

She seemed to enjoy his confusion; she was cruel enough to repeat the question. Tell me, Edmund, and truly, do you wish to see me give my hand to Wenlock? I insist upon your answer.—All on a sudden he recovered both his voice and courage; he stepped forward, his person erect, his countenance assured, his voice resolute and intrepid.—Since Lady Emma insists upon my answer, since she avows a dislike to Wenlock, since she condescends to ask my opinion, I will tell her my thoughts, my wishes. The fair Emma now trembled in her turn; she blushed, looked down, and was ashamed to have spoken so freely. Edmund went on: My most ardent wishes are, that the fair Emma may reserve her heart and hand till a certain person, a friend of mine, is at liberty to solicit them; whose utmost ambition is, first to deserve, and then to obtain them.—Your friend, Sir! said Lady Emma; her brow clouded, her eye disdainful. Edmund proceeded: My friend is so particularly circumstanced that he cannot at present with propriety ask for Lady Emma's favour; but as soon as he has gained a cause that is yet in suspence, he will openly declare his pretensions, and if he is unsuccessful he will then condemn himself to eternal silence. Lady Emma knew not what to think of this declaration, she hoped, she feared, she meditated; but her attention was too strongly excited to be satisfied without some gratification: After a pause, she pursued the subject. And this friend of yours, Sir, of what degree and fortune is he? Edmund smiled; but, commanding his emotion, he replied, his birth is noble, his degree and fortune uncertain. Her countenance fell, she sighed; he proceeded. It is utterly impossible, said he, for any man of inferior degree to aspire to Lady Emma's favour; her noble birth, the dignity of her beauty and virtues, must awe and keep at their proper distance, all men of inferior degree and merit; they may admire, they may revere; but they must not presume to approach too near, lest their presumption should meet with its punishment.—Well, Sir, said she, suddenly; and so this friend of yours has commissioned you to speak in his behalf?—He has, Madam.—Then I must tell you, that I think his assurance is very great, and yours not much less.—I am sorry for that, Madam.—Tell him, that I shall reserve my heart and hand for the man to whom my father shall bid me give them.—Very well, Lady; I am certain my Lord loves you too well to dispose of them against your inclination.—How do you know that, Sir? But tell him that the man that hopes for my favour must apply to my Lord for his.—That is my friend's intention, his resolution I should say, as soon as he can do it with propriety; and I accept your permission for him to do so.—My permission did you say? I am astonished at your assurance! tell me no more of your friend: But perhaps you are pleading for Wenlock all this time: It is all one to me; only, say no more.—Are you offended with me, Madam?—No matter, Sir.—Yes, it is.—I am surprised at you, Edmund!—I am surprised at my own temerity; but, forgive me.—It does not signify; good bye ty'e, Sir.—Don't leave me in anger, Madam; I cannot bear that: Perhaps I may not see you again for a long time? He looked afflicted; she turned back. I do forgive you, Edmund: I was concerned for you; but, it seems, you are more concerned for every body than for yourself. She sighed: Farewell! said she.— Edmund gazed on her with tenderness; he approached her, he just touched her hand; his heart was rising to his lips, but he recollected his situation; he checked himself immediately; he retired back, he sighed deeply, bowed low, and hastily quitted her.

The Lady turning into another walk, he reached the house first, and went up again to his chamber; he threw himself upon his knees; prayed for a thousand blessings upon every one of the family of his benefactor, and involuntarily wept at mentioning the name of the charming Emma, whom he was about to leave abruptly, and perhaps for ever. He then endeavoured to compose himself and once more attended the Baron; wished him a good night; and withdrew to his chamber, till he was called upon to go again to the haunted apartment.

He came down equipped for his journey, and went hastily for fear of observation; he paid his customary devotions, and soon after Oswald tapped at the door. They conferred together upon the interesting subject that engrossed their attention, until Joseph came to them; who brought the rest of Edmund's baggage, and some refreshment for him before he set out. Edmund promised to give them the earliest information of his situation and success. At the hour of twelve they heard the same groans as the night before in the lower apartment; but, being somewhat familiarized to it, they were not so strongly affected: Oswald crossed himself, and prayed for the departed soul; he also prayed for Edmund, and recommended him to the divine protection: He then arose, and embraced that young man; who, also, took a tender leave of his friend Joseph. They then went, with silence and caution, through a long gallery; they descended the stairs in the same manner; they crossed the hall in profound silence, and hardly dared to breathe lest they should be overheard: They found some difficulty in opening one of the folding doors, which at last they accomplished; they were again in jeopardy at the outward gate; at length they conveyed him safely into the stables: There they again embraced him, and prayed for his prosperity.

He then mounted his horse and set forward to Wyatt's cottage; he hallowed at the door, and was answered from within: In a few minutes John came out to him.—What, is it you, Master Edmund?—Hush! said he; not a word of who I am: I go upon private business, and would not wish to be known.—If you will go forward, Sir, I will soon overtake you: He did so; and they pursued their journey to the north. In the mean time, Oswald and Joseph returned in silence into the house; they retired to their respective apartments without hearing or being heard by any one.

About the dawn of day Oswald intended to lay his pacquets in the way of those to whom they were addressed; after much contrivance he determined to take a bold step, and, if he were discovered, to frame some excuse. Encouraged by his late success, he went on tip-toe into Master William's chamber, placed a letter upon his pillow, and withdrew unheard. Exulting in his heart, he attempted the Baron's apartment, but found it fastened within; finding this scheme frustrated, he waited till the hour the Baron was expected down to breakfast, and laid the letter and the key of the haunted apartment upon the table.

Soon after, he saw the Baron enter the breakfast room; he got out of sight, but staid within call, preparing himself for a summons. The Baron sat down to breakfast; he saw a letter directed to himself, he opened it, and to his great surprise, read as follows:

'The guardian of the haunted apartment to Baron Fitz-Owen. To thee I remit the key of my charge, until the right owner shall come, who will both discover and avenge my wrongs; then, woe be to the guilty! But let the innocent rest in peace. In the mean time, let none presume to explore the secrets of my apartment, lest they suffer for their temerity.'

The Baron was struck with amazement at the letter: He took up the key, examined it, then laid it down, and took up the letter; he was in such confusion of thought, he knew not what to do or say for several minutes: At length he called his servants about him; the first question he asked was,—Where is Edmund?— They could not tell.—Has he been called?—Yes, my Lord, but nobody answered, and the key was not in the door.—Where is Joseph?—Gone into the stables.—Where is Father Oswald?—In his study.—Seek him, and desire him to come hither.—By the time the Baron had read the letter over again, he came.

He had been framing a steady countenance to answer to all interrogatories; as he came in he attentively observed the Baron, whose features were in strong agitation; as soon as he saw Oswald, he spoke as one out of breath.—Take that key, and read this letter!—He did so, shrugged up his shoulders, and remained silent.—Father, said my Lord, what think you of this letter?—It is a very surprising one.—The contents are alarming; where is Edmund?—I do not know.—Has nobody seen him?—Not that I know of.—Call my sons, my kinsmen, my servants.—The servants came in.—Have any of you seen or heard of Edmund?— No, was the answer.—Father, step up stairs to my sons and kinsmen, and desire them to come down immediately.

Oswald withdrew; and went first to Mr. William's chamber. My dear Sir, you must come to my Lord now directly; he has something extraordinary to communicate to you.—And so have I, Father; see what I have found upon my pillow!—Pray, Sir, read it to me before you shew it to any body; my Lord is alarmed too much already, and wants nothing to increase his consternation. William read his letter, while Oswald looked as if he was an utter stranger to the contents, which were these:

'Whatever may be heard or seen, let the seal of friendship be upon thy lips. The peasant Edmund is no more: But there still lives a man who hopes to acknowledge, and repay, the Lord Fitz-Owen's generous care and protection; to return his beloved

William's vowed affection, and to claim his friendship on terms of equality.'

What, said William, can this mean?—It is not easy to say, replied Oswald.—Can you tell what is the cause of this alarm?—I can tell you nothing, but that my Lord desires to see you directly; pray make haste down; I must go up to your brothers and kinsmen: Nobody knows what to think, or believe.

Master William went down stairs, and Father Oswald went to the malecontents: As soon as he entered the outward door of their apartment, Mr. Wenlock called out—Here comes the friend; now for some new proposal!—Gentlemen, said Oswald, my Lord desires your company immediately in the breakfast parlour.— What! to meet your favourite Edmund, I suppose? said Mr. Wenlock.—No, Sir.—What, then, is the matter? said Sir Robert.—Something very extraordinary has happened, gentlemen: Edmund is not to be found; he disappeared from the haunted apartment, the key of which was conveyed to my Lord in a strange manner, with a letter from an unknown hand: My Lord is both surprised and concerned, and wishes to have your opinion and advice on the occasion.—Tell him, said Sir Robert, we will wait upon him immediately.

As Oswald went away, he heard Wenlock say,—So Edmund is gone, it is no matter how, or whither.—Another said, I hope the ghost has taken him out of the way. The rest laughed at the conceit, as they followed Oswald down stairs.—They found the Baron, and his son William, commenting upon the key and the letter. My Lord gave them to Sir Robert, who looked on them with marks of surprise and confusion. The Baron addressed him: Is not this a very strange affair? Son Robert, lay aside your ill humours, and behave to your father with the respect and affection his tenderness deserves from you, and give me your advice and opinion on this alarming subject.—My Lord, said Sir Robert, I am as much confounded as yourself: I can give no advice: Let my cousins see the letter; let us have their opinion. They read it in turn; they were equally surprised: But when it came into Wenlock's hand, he paused and mediated some minutes; at length—I am indeed surprised, and still more concerned, to see my Lord and Uncle the dupe of an artful contrivance; and, if he will permit me, I shall endeavour to unriddle it, to the confusion of all that are concerned in it.—Do so, Dick, said my Lord, and you shall have my thanks for it.—This letter, said he, I imagine to be the contrivance of Edmund, or some ingenious friend of his, to conceal some designs they have against the peace of this family, which has been too often disturbed upon that rascal's account.—But what end could be proposed by it? said the Baron.—Why, one part of the scheme is to cover Edmund's departure, that is clear enough; for the rest, we can only guess at it: Perhaps he may be concealed somewhere in that apartment, from whence he may rush out in the night, and either rob or murder us, or, at least, alarm and terrify the family.—The Baron smiled: You shoot beyond the mark, Sir, and overshoot yourself, as you have done before now; you shew only your inveteracy against that poor lad, whom you cannot mention with temper: To what purpose should he shut himself up there, to be starved?—Starved! no, no! he has friends in this house (looking at Oswald), who will not suffer him to want any thing: Those who have always magnified his virtues, and extenuated his faults, will lend a hand to help him in time of need; and perhaps, to assist his ingenious contrivances.—Oswald shrugged up his shoulders, and remained silent. This is a strange fancy of yours, Dick, said my Lord; but I am willing to pursue it; first, to discover what you drive at; and, secondly, to satisfy all that are here present of the truth or falsehood of it, that they may know what value to set upon your sagacity hereafter. Let us all go over that apartment together; and let Joseph be called to attend us thither. Oswald offered to call him, but Wenlock stopped him. No, Father, said he, you must stay with us; we want your ghostly counsel and advice: Joseph shall have no private conference with you.—What mean you, said Oswald, to insinuate to my Lord against me, or Joseph? But your ill-will spares nobody. It will one day be known who is the disturber of the peace of this family; I wait for that time, and am silent.

Joseph came; when he was told whither they were going, he looked hard at Oswald. Wenlock observed them: Lead the way,

Father! said he; and Joseph shall follow us. Oswald smiled: We will go where Heaven permits us, said he; alas! the wisdom of man can neither hasten, nor retard, its decrees.

They followed the Father up stairs, and went directly to the haunted apartment. The Baron unlocked the door; he bid Joseph open the shutters and admit the day-light, which had been excluded for many years. They went over the rooms above stairs, and then descended the staircase, and through the lower rooms in the same manner. However, they overlooked the closet in which the fatal secret was concealed; the door was covered with tapestry the same as the room, and united so well that it seemed but one piece. Wenlock tauntingly desired Father Oswald to introduce them to the ghost. The Father in reply, asked them where they should find Edmund? Do you think, said he, that he lies hid in my pocket, or in Joseph's?—'Tis no matter, answered he; thoughts are free.—My opinion of you, Sir, said Oswald, is not founded upon thoughts: I judge of men by their actions; a rule, I believe, it will not suit you to be tried by.—None of your insolent admonitions, Father! returned Wenlock; this is neither the time nor the place for them.—That is truer than you are aware of, Sir; I meant not to enter into the subject just now.—Be silent, said my Lord.—I shall enter into this subject with you hereafter; then look you be prepared for it! In the mean time do you, Dick Wenlock, answer to my questions. Do you think Edmund is concealed in this apartment?—No, Sir.—Do you think there is any mystery in it?—No, my Lord.—Is it haunted, think you?—No, I think not.—Should you be afraid to try?—In what manner, my Lord?—Why, you have shewn your wit upon the subject, and I mean to shew your courage; you, and Jack Markham your confident, shall sleep here three nights as Edmund has done before.—Sir, said Sir Robert, for what purpose? I should be glad to understand why?—I have my reasons, Sir, as well as your kinsmen there. No reply, Sirs! I insist upon being obeyed in this point. Joseph, let the beds be well aired, and every thing made agreeable to the Gentlemen: If there is any contrivance to impose upon me, they, I am sure, will have pleasure in detecting it; and, if not, I shall obtain my end in making these rooms habitable.

Oswald come with me, and the rest may go where they list till dinner-time.

The Baron went with Oswald into the parlour. Now tell me, Father, said he, do you disapprove what I have done?—Quite the contrary, my Lord, said he; I entirely approve it.—But you do not know all my reasons for it. Yesterday Edmund's behaviour was different from what I have ever seen it; he is naturally frank and open in all his ways; but he was then silent, thoughtful, absent; he sighed deeply, and once I saw tears stand in his eyes: Now, I do suspect there is something uncommon in that apartment; that Edmund has discovered the secret; and, fearing to disclose it, he is fled away from the house. As to this letter, perhaps he may have written it to hint that there is more than he dares reveal; I tremble at the hints contained in it, though I shall appear to make light of it: But I and mine are innocent; and if Heaven discloses the guilt of others, I ought to adore and submit to its decrees.—That is prudently and piously resolved, my Lord; let us do our duty, and leave events to Heaven.—But, Father, I have a further view in obliging my kinsmen to sleep there: If any thing should appear to them, it is better that it should only be known to my own family; if there is nothing in it, I shall put to the proof the courage and veracity of my two kinsmen, of whom I think very indifferently. I mean shortly to enquire into many things I have heard lately to their disadvantage; and, if I find them guilty, they shall not escape with impunity.—My Lord, said Oswald, you judge like yourself; I wish you to make enquiry concerning them, and believe the result will be to their confusion, and your Lordship will be enabled to re-establish the peace of your family.

During this conversation, Oswald was upon his guard, lest any thing should escape that might create suspicion. He withdrew as soon as he could with decency, and left the Baron meditating what all these things should mean: He feared there was some misfortune impending over his house, though he knew not from what cause.

He dined with his children and kinsmen, and strove to appear chearful; but a gloom was perceivable through his deportment. Sir Robert was reserved and respectful; Mr. William was silent and attentive; the rest of the family dutifully assiduous to my Lord; only Wenlock and Markham were sullen and chagrined. The Baron detained the young men the whole afternoon; he strove to amuse and to be amused; he shewed the greatest affection and parental regard to his children, and endeavoured to conciliate their affections, and engage their gratitude by kindness. Wenlock and Markham felt their courage abate as the night approached: At the hour of nine old Joseph came to conduct them to the haunted apartment; they took leave of their kinsmen, and went up stairs with heavy hearts.

They found the chamber set in order for them, and a table spread with provision and good liquor to keep up their spirits. It seems, said Wenlock, that your friend Edmund was obliged to you for his accommodations here.—Sir, said Joseph, his accommodations were bad enough the first night; but, afterwards, they were bettered by my Lord's orders.—Owing to your officious cares? said Wenlock: I own it, said Joseph, and I am not ashamed of it.— Are you not anxious to know what is become of him? said Markham.—Not at all, Sir; I trust he is in the best protection; so good a young man as he is, is safe every where.—You see cousin Jack, said Wenlock, how this villain has stole the hearts of my Uncle's servants: I suppose this canting old fellow knows where he is, if the truth were known.—Have you any further commands for me, Gentlemen? said the old man.—No, not we.—Then I am ordered to attend my Lord when you have done with me.—Go, then, about your business. Joseph went away, glad to be dismissed.

What shall we do, cousin Jack, said Wenlock, to pass away the time? it is plaguy dull sitting here.—Dull enough, said Markham; I think the best thing we can do is to go to bed and sleep it away.—Faith, says Wenlock, I am in no disposition to sleep! Who would have thought the old man would have obliged us to spend the night here?—Don't say *us*, I beg of you, it was all your own doing, replied Markham.—I did not intend he should have taken me at my word.—Then you should have spoken more cautiously. I have always been governed by you, like a fool as I am; you play the braggart, and I suffer for it: But they begin to see through your fine-spun arts and contrivances, and I believe you will meet with your deserts one day or other.—What now! do you mean to affront me, Jack? know, that some are born to plan, others to execute; I am one of the former, thou of the latter: Know your friend, or—Or what? replied Markham; do you mean to threaten me? If you do!—What then? said Wenlock.—Why, then, I will try which of us two is the best man, Sir! Upon this Markham arose, and put himself into a posture of defence. Wenlock perceiving he was serious in his anger, began to sooth him; he persuaded, he flattered, he promised great things if he would be composed. Markham was sullen, uneasy, resentful; whenever he spoke it was to upbraid Wenlock with his treachery and falsehood. Wenlock tried all his eloquence to get him into a good humour, but in vain; he threatened to acquaint his Uncle with all that he knew, and to exculpate himself at the other's expence. Wenlock began to find his choler rise; they were both almost choaked with rage; and, at length, they both rose with a resolution to fight.

As they stood with their fists clenched, on a sudden they were alarmed with a dismal groan from the room underneath. They stood like statues petrified by fear, yet listening with trembling expectation: A second groan increased their consternation; and, soon after, a third compleated it. They staggered to a seat, and sunk down upon it, ready to faint; presently all the doors flew open, a pale glimmering light appeared at the door from the staircase, and a man in compleat armour entered the room: He stood with one hand extended,* pointing to the outward door; they took the hint, and crawled away as fast as fear would let them; they staggered along the gallery, and from thence to the Baron's apartment, where Wenlock sunk down in a swoon, and Markham had just strength enough to knock at the door.

The servant who slept in the outward room alarmed his Lord: Markham cried out—For Heaven's sake, let us in! Upon hearing his voice, the door was opened, and Markham approached his Uncle in such an attitude of fear, as excited a degree of it in the Baron. He pointed to Wenlock, who was with some difficulty recovered from the fit he was fallen into; the servant was terrified, he rung the alarm bell; the servants came running from all parts to their Lord's apartment: The young Gentlemen came likewise, and presently all was confusion, and the terror was universal. Oswald, who guessed the business, was the only one that could question them; he asked, several times,—What is the matter?— Markham, at last, answered him: We have seen the ghost!—All regard to secrecy was now at an end; the echo ran through the whole family:—They have seen the ghost!

The Baron desired Oswald to talk to the young men, and endeavour to quiet the disturbance. He came forward; he comforted some, he rebuked others; he bad the servants retire into the outward room: The Baron, with his sons and kinsmen, remained in the bed-chamber. It is very unfortunate, said Oswald, that this affair should be made so public; surely these young men might have related what they had seen without alarming the whole family: I am very much concerned upon my Lord's account.—I thank you, Father, said the Baron; but prudence was quite overthrown here: Wenlock was half dead, and Markham half distracted; the family were alarmed without my being able to prevent it: But let us hear what these poor terrified creatures say. Oswald demanded, What have you seen, Gentlemen?—The ghost! said Markham.—In what form did it appear?—A man in armour.—Did it speak to you?—No.—What did it do to terrify you so much?—It stood at the farthest door, and pointed to the outward door, as if to have us leave the room; we did not wait for a second notice, but came away as fast as we could.—Did it follow you?—No.—Then you need not have raised such a disturbance. Wenlock lifted up his head, and spoke: I believe, Father, if you had been with us, you would not have stood upon ceremonies any more than we did. I wish my Lord would send you to parley with the ghost; for, without doubt, you are better qualified than we.— My Lord, said Oswald, I will go thither with your permission; I will see that every thing is safe, and bring the key back to you: Perhaps this may help to dispel the fears that have been raised; at least, I will try to do it.—I thank you, Father, for your good offices; do as you please.

Oswald went into the outward room. I am going, said he, to shut up the apartment: The young Gentlemen have been more frightened than they had occasion for; I will try to account for it. Which of you will go with me? They all drew back, except Joseph, who offered to bear him company. They went into the bedroom in the haunted apartment, and found every thing quiet there. They put out the fire, extinguished the lights, locked the door, and brought away the key. As they returned, I thought how it would be, said Joseph.—Hush! not a word, said Oswald; you find we are suspected of something, though they know not what. Wait till you are called upon, and then we will both speak to purpose. They carried the key to the Baron.

All is quiet in the apartment, said Oswald, as we can testify.— Did you ask Joseph to go with you, said the Baron, or did he offer himself?—My Lord, I asked if any body would go with me, and they all declined it but he; I thought proper to have a witness beside myself, for whatever might be seen or heard.—Joseph, you was servant to the late Lord Lovel; what kind of man was he?—A very comely man, please your Lordship.—Should you know him if you were to see him?—I cannot say, my Lord.—Would you have any objection to sleep a night in that apartment?—I beg,—I hope,—I beseech your Lordship not to command me to do it!— You are then afraid; why did you offer yourself to go thither?— Because I was not so much frightened as the rest.—I wish you would lay a night there; but, I do not insist upon it.—My Lord, I am a poor ignorant old man, not fit for such an undertaking: Beside, if I should see the ghost, and if it should be the person of my Master, and if it should tell me any thing, and bid me keep it secret, I should not dare to disclose it; and then, what service should I do your Lordship?—That is true, indeed, said the Baron.

This speech, said Sir Robert, is both a simple and an artful one: You see, however, that Joseph is not a man for us to depend upon; he regards the Lord Lovel, though dead, more than Lord Fitz-Owen, living; he calls him his Master, and promises to keep his secrets. What say you, Father, is the ghost your Master, or your friend? Are you under any obligation to keep his secrets?— Sir, said Oswald, I answer as Joseph does; I would sooner die than discover a secret revealed in that manner.—I thought as much, said Sir Robert; there is a mystery in Father Oswald's behaviour that I cannot comprehend.—Do not reflect upon the Father, said the Baron, I have no cause to complain of him; perhaps the mystery may be too soon explained: But let us not anticipate evils. Oswald and Joseph have spoken like good men; I am satisfied with their answers: Let us, who are innocent, rest in peace; and let us endeavour to restore peace in the family; and do you, Father, assist us:—With my best services, said Oswald. He called the servants in: Let nothing be mentioned out of doors, said he, of what has lately passed within, especially in the east apartment; the young Gentlemen had not so much reason to be frightened as they apprehended; a piece of furniture fell down in the rooms underneath, which made the noise that alarmed them so much: But I can certify that all things in the rooms are in quiet, and there is nothing to fear. All of you attend me in the chapel in an hour; do your duties, put your trust in God, and obey your Lord, and you will find every thing go right as it used to do.

They dispersed; the sun rose, the day came on, and every thing went on in the usual course: But the servants were not so easily satisfied; they whispered that something was wrong, and expected the time that should set all right.—The mind of the Baron was employed in meditating upon these circumstances that seemed to him the forerunners of some great events: He sometimes thought of Edmund; he sighed for his expulsion, and lamented the uncertainty of his fate; but, to his family, he appeared easy and satisfied.

From the time of Edmund's departure the fair Emma had many uneasy hours; she wished to enquire after him, but feared to show any solicitude concerning him: The next day, when her brother William came into her apartment, she took courage to ask a question. Pray, brother, can you give any guess what is become of Edmund?—No, said he (with a sigh), why do you ask me?— Because, my dear William, I should think if any body knew, it must be you; and I thought he loved you too well to leave you in ignorance: But don't you think he left the Castle in a very strange manner?—I do, my dear; there is a mystery in every circumstance of his departure: Nevertheless (I will trust you with a secret), he did not leave the Castle without making a distinction in my favour.—I thought so, said she; but you might tell *me* what you know about him?—Alas, my dear Emma! I know nothing: When I saw him last he seemed a good deal affected, as if he were taking leave of me; and I had a foreboding that we parted for a longer time than usual.—Ah! so had I, said she, when he parted from me in the garden.—What leave did he take of you, Emma?—She blushed, and hesitated to tell him all that passed between them; but he begged, persuaded, insisted, and, at length, under the strongest injunctions of secrecy, she told him all. He said, that Edmund's behaviour on that occasion was as mysterious as the rest of his conduct; but now you have revealed your secret, you have a right to know mine. He then gave her the letter he found upon his pillow; she read it with great emotion. Saint Winifred* assist me! said she; what can I think? 'The peasant Edmund is no more, but there lives one,'—that is to my thinking, Edmund lives, but is no peasant.—Go on, my dear, said William; I like your explanation.—Nay, brother, I only guess; but what think you?—I believe we think alike in more than one respect, that he meant to recommend no other person than himself to your favour; and, if he were indeed of noble birth, I would prefer him to a prince for a husband to my Emma!—Bless me! said she, do you think it possible that he should be of either birth or fortune?—It is hard to say what is impossible! We have proof that the east apartment is haunted: It was there that Edmund was made acquainted with many secrets, I doubt not; and perhaps his own fate may be involved in that of others. I am confident that what he saw and heard there, was the cause of his departure. We must wait with patience the unravelling this intricate affair: I believe I need not enjoin your secrecy as to what I have said, your heart will be my security.—What mean you brother?—Don't affect ignorance, my dear; you love Edmund, so do I; it is nothing to be ashamed of: It would have been strange if a girl of your good sense had not distinguished a swan among a flock of geese.—Dear William, don't let a word of this escape you; but you have taken a weight off my heart. You may depend that I will not dispose of my hand or heart till I know the end of this affair. William smiled: Keep them for Edmund's *friend*: I shall rejoice to see him in a situation to ask them.—Hush, my brother! not a word more, I hear footsteps. They were her eldest brother's, who came to ask Mr. William to ride out with him, which finished the conference.

The fair Emma from this time assumed an air of satisfaction; and William frequently stole away from his companions to talk with his sister upon their favourite subject.

While these things passed at the Castle of Lovel, Edmund and his companion John Wyatt proceeded on their journey to Sir Philip Harclay's seat; they conversed together on the way, and Edmund found him a man of understanding, though not improved by education; he also discovered that John loved his Master and respected him even to veneration; from him he learned many particulars concerning that worthy Knight. Wyatt told him, that Sir Philip maintained twelve old soldiers who had been maimed and disabled in the wars, and had no provision made for them; also six old officers who had been unfortunate and were grown grey without preferment; he likewise mentioned the Greek Gentleman, his master's captive and friend, as a man eminent for valour and piety; but, beside these, said Wyatt, there are many others who eat of my Master's bread and drink of his cup, and who join in blessings and prayers to Heaven for their noble benefactor; his ears are ever open to distress, his hand to relieve it, and he shares in every good man's joys and blessings.— Oh what a glorious character! said Edmund: how my heart throbs with wishes to imitate such a man! Oh that I might resemble him, though at ever so great a distance! Edmund was never weary of hearing the actions of this truly great man, nor Wyatt with relating them; and during three days' journey, there were but few pauses in their conversation.

The fourth day, when they came within view of the house, Edmund's heart began to raise doubts of his reception. If, said he, Sir Philip should not receive me kindly, if he should resent my long neglect, and disown my acquaintance, it would be no more than justice.

He sent Wyatt before to notify his arrival to Sir Philip, while he waited at the gate, full of doubts and anxieties concerning his reception. Wyatt was met and congratulated on his return by most of his fellow-servants; he asked, where is my master?—In the parlour.—Are any strangers with him?—No, only his own family.—Then I will shew myself to him. He presented himself before Sir Philip. So John, said he, you are welcome home! I hope you left your parents and relations well?—All well, thank God! and send their humble duty to your honour, and they pray for you every day of their lives; I hope your honour is in good health?—Very well.—Thank God for that! but, Sir, I have something further to tell you: I have had a companion all the way home, a person who comes to wait on your honour on business of great consequence, as he says.—Who is that, John?—It is Master Edmund Twyford, from the Castle of Lovel.—Young Edmund! says Sir Philip, surprised: Where is he?—At the gate, Sir.—Why did you leave him there?—Because he bad me come before, and acquaint your honour, that he waits your pleasure.—Bring him hither, said Sir Philip; tell him I shall be glad to see him.

John made haste to deliver his message, and Edmund followed him in silence into Sir Philip's presence: He bowed low, and kept at distance. Sir Philip held out his hand and bad him approach. As he drew near he was seized with an universal trembling; he kneeled down, took his hand, kissed it, and pressed it to his heart in silence.

You are welcome, young man! said Sir Philip; take courage, and speak for yourself. Edmund sighed deeply; he at length broke silence with difficulty. I am come thus far, noble Sir, to throw myself at your feet, and implore your protection. You are, under God, my only reliance!—I receive you, said Sir Philip, with all my heart! Your person is greatly improved since I saw you last, and I hope your mind is equally so: I have heard a great character of you from some that knew you in France. I remember the promise I made you long ago, and am ready now to fulfil it, upon condition that you have done nothing, to disgrace the good opinion I formerly entertained of you; and am ready to serve you in any thing consistent with my own honour. Edmund kissed the hand that was extended to raise him. I accept your favour, Sir, upon this condition only; and if ever you find me to impose upon your

credulity, or incroach on your goodness, may you renounce me
from that moment!—Enough, said Sir Philip; rise, then, and let
me embrace you: You are truly welcome!—Oh, noble Sir! said
Edmund, I have a strange story to tell you; but it must be by
ourselves, with only Heaven to bear witness to what passes
between us.—Very well, said Sir Philip; I am ready to hear you:
But first, go and get some refreshment after your journey, and
then come to me again; John Wyatt will attend you.—I want no
refreshment, said Edmund; and I cannot eat or drink till I have
told my business to your honour.—Well then, said Sir Philip,
come along with me. He took the youth by the hand and led him
into another parlour, leaving his friends in great surprize, what
this young man's errand could be: John Wyatt told them all that
he knew relating to Edmund's birth, character, and situation.

When Sir Philip had seated his young friend, he listened in
silence to the surprizing tale he had to tell him. Edmund told him
briefly the most remarkable circumstances of his life, from the
time when he first saw and liked him, till his return from France;
but from that æra he related at large every thing that had happened, recounting every interesting particular which was
imprinted on his memory in strong and lasting characters.—Sir
Philip grew every moment more affected by the recital; sometimes he clasped his hands together, he lifted them up to heaven,
he smote his breast, he sighed, he exclaimed aloud; when
Edmund related his dream, he breathed short, and seemed to
devour him with attention; when he described the fatal closet, he
trembled, sighed, sobbed, and was almost suffocated with his
agitations: But when he related all that passed between his supposed mother and himself, and finally produced the jewels, the
proofs of his birth, and the death of his unfortunate mother—he
flew to him, he pressed him to his bosom, he strove to speak, but
speech was for some minutes denied: He wept aloud; and, at
length, his words found their way in broken exclamations.—Son
of my dearest friend!—dear and precious relick of a noble
house!—child of providence!—the beloved of heaven!—
welcome! thrice welcome to my arms!—to my heart!—I will be
thy parent from henceforward, and thou shalt be indeed my child,

my heir! My mind told me from the first moment I beheld thee, that thou wert the image of my friend! my heart then opened itself to receive thee, as his offspring. I had a strange foreboding that I was to be thy protector. I would then have made thee my own; but heaven orders things for the best; it made thee the instrument of this discovery, and in its own time and manner conducted thee to my arms. Praise be to God for his wonderful doings towards the children of men! every thing that has befallen thee is by his direction, and he will not leave his work unfinished; I trust that I shall be his instrument to do justice on the guilty, and to restore the orphan of my friend to his rights and title. I devote myself to this service, and will make it the business of my life to effect it.

Edmund gave vent to his emotions, in raptures of joy and gratitude. They spent several hours in this way, without thinking of the time that passed; the one enquiring, the other explaining, and repeating, every particular of the interesting story.

At length they were interrupted by the careful John Wyatt, who was anxious to know if any thing was likely to give trouble to his Master. Sir, said John, it grows dark, do you want a light?—We want no light but what heaven gives us, said Sir Philip; I knew not whether it was dark or light.—I hope, said John, nothing has happened, I hope your honour has heard no bad tidings,—I—I—I hope no offence.—None at all, said the good Knight, I am obliged to your solicitude for me: I have heard some things that grieve me, and others that give me great pleasure; but the sorrows are past, and the joys remain.—Thank God! said John; I was afraid something was the matter to give your honour trouble.—I thank you, my good servant! You see this young gentleman; I would have you, John, devote yourself to his service: I give you to him for an attendant on his person, and would have you show your affection to me by your attachment to him.—Oh, Sir! said John in a melancholy voice, what have I done to be turned out of your service?—No such matter, John, said Sir Philip; you will not leave my service.—Sir, said John, I would rather die than leave you.—And, my lad, I like you too well to part with you; but in serving my friend, you will serve me: Know, that this young man is my son.—Your son, Sir! said John!—Not my natural son, but my relation; my son by adoption, my heir!—And will he live with you, Sir?—Yes, John; and I hope to die with him.—Oh, then, I will serve him with all my heart and soul; and I will do my best to please you both.—I thank you, John, and I will not forget your honest love and duty: I have so good an opinion of you, that I will tell you of some things concerning this gentleman that will entitle him to your respect.—'Tis enough for me, said John, to know that your honour respects him, to make me pay him as much duty as yourself.—But, John, when you know him better, you will respect him still more; at present, I shall only tell you what he is not; for you think him only the son of Andrew Twyford.—And is he not? said John.—No; but his wife nursed him, and he passed for her son.—And does old Twyford know it, Sir?—He does, and will bear witness to it; but he is the son of a near friend of mine, of quality superior to my own, and as such you must serve and respect him.—I shall to be sure, Sir; but what name shall I call him?—You shall know that hereafter; in the mean time bring a light, and wait on us to the other parlour.

When John was withdrawn, Sir Philip said, that is a point to be considered and determined immediately: It is proper that you should assume a name till you can take that of your father; for I choose you should drop that of your foster father; and I would have you be called by one that is respectable.—In that, and every other point, I will be wholly governed by you, Sir, said Edmund.—Well then, I will give you the name of Seagrave: I shall say that you are a relation of my own; and my mother was really of that family.

John soon returned, and attended them into the other parlour: Sir Philip entered, with Edmund in his hand.—My friends, said he, this gentleman is Mr. Edmund Seagrave, the son of a dear friend and relation of mine: He was lost in his infancy, brought up by a good woman out of pure humanity, and is but lately restored to his own family: The circumstances shall be made known hereafter: In the mean time, I have taken him under my care and protection, and will use all my power and interest to see him restored to his fortune, which is enjoyed by the usurper who was the cause of his expulsion, and the death of his parents. Receive him as my relation, and friend: Zadisky, do you embrace him first! Edmund, you and this gentleman must love each other for my sake; hereafter you will do it for your own. They all rose, each embraced and congratulated the young man. Zadisky said, Sir, whatever griefs and misfortunes you may have endured, you may reckon them at an end, from the hour you are beloved, and protected by Sir Philip Harclay.—I firmly believe it, Sir, replied Edmund; and my heart enjoys, already, more happiness than I ever yet felt, and promises me all that I can wish in future: His friendship is the earnest Heaven gives me of its blessings hereafter.

They sat down to supper with mutual chearfulness; and Edmund enjoyed the repast with more satisfaction than he had felt a long time. Sir Philip saw his countenance brighten up, and looked on him with heart-felt pleasure. Every time I look on you, said he, reminds me of your father; you are the same person I loved twenty-three years ago: I rejoice to see you under my roof. Go to your repose early, and to-morrow we will consult farther. Edmund withdrew, and enjoyed a night of sweet undisturbed repose.

The next morning Edmund arose in perfect health and spirits; he waited on his benefactor. They were soon after joined by Zadisky, who shewed great attention and respect to the youth, and offered him his best services without reserve. Edmund accepted them with equal respect and modesty; and finding himself at ease, began to display his amiable qualities. They breakfasted together; afterwards, Sir Philip desired Edmund to walk out with him.

As soon as they were out of hearing, Sir Philip said, I could not sleep last night for thinking of your affairs: I laid schemes for you, and rejected them again. We must lay our plan before we begin to act. What shall be done with this treacherous kinsman! this inhuman monster! this assassin of his nearest relation? I will risk my life and fortune to bring him to justice. Shall I go to court, and demand justice of the King? or shall I accuse him of the murder, and make him stand a publick trial? If I treat him as a

Baron of the realm, he must be tried by his peers; if as a com-
moner, he must be tried at the county assize: But we must shew
reason why he should be degraded from his title. Have you any
thing to propose?—Nothing, Sir; I have only to wish that it might
be as private as possible, for the sake of my noble benefactor, the
Lord Fitz-Owen, upon whom some part of the family disgrace
would naturally fall; and that would be an ill return for all his
kindness and generosity to me.—That is a generous and grateful
consideration on your part; but you owe still more to the memory
of your injured parents. However, there is yet another way that
suits me better than any hitherto proposed: I will challenge the
traitor to meet me in the field; and, if he has spirit enough to
answer my call, I will there bring him to justice; if not, I will
bring him to a publick trial.

No, Sir, said Edmund, that is my province: Should I stand by
and see my noble gallant friend expose his life for me, I should be
unworthy to bear the name of that friend whom you so much
lament. It will become his son to vindicate his name, and revenge
his death. I will be the challenger, and no other.—And do you
think he will answer the challenge of an unknown youth, with
nothing but his pretensions to his name and title? Certainly not.
Leave this matter to me: I think of a way that will oblige him to
meet me at the house of a third person who is known to all the
parties concerned, and where we will have authentick witnesses
of all that passes between him and me. I will devise the time,
place, and manner, and satisfy all your scruples. Edmund offered
to reply; but Sir Philip bad him be silent, and let him proceed in
his own way.

He then led him over his estate, and shewed him every thing
deserving his notice; he told him all the particulars of his domes-
tick œconomy, and they returned home in time to meet their
friends at dinner.

They spent several days in consulting how to bring Sir Walter
to account, and in improving their friendship and confidence in
each other. Edmund endeared himself so much to his friend and
patron, that he declared him his adopted son and heir before all
his friends and servants, and ordered them to respect him as such.

He every day improved their love and regard for him, and became the darling of the whole family.

After much consideration, Sir Philip fixed his resolutions, and began to execute his purposes. He set out for the seat of the Lord Clifford, attended by Edmund, M. Zadisky, and two servants. Lord Clifford received them with kindness and hospitality.

Sir Philip presented Edmund to Lord Clifford and his family, as his near relation and presumptive heir: They spent the evening in the pleasures of convivial mirth and hospitable entertainment. The next day Sir Philip began to open his mind to Lord Clifford, informing him that both his young friend and himself had received great injuries from the present Lord Lovel, for which they were resolved to call him to account; but that, for many reasons, they were desirous to have proper witnesses of all that should pass between them, and begging the favour of his Lordship to be the principal one. Lord Clifford acknowledged the confidence placed in him; and besought Sir Philip to let him be the arbitrator between them. Sir Philip assured him, that their wrongs would not admit of arbitration, as he should hereafter judge; but that he was unwilling to explain them further till he knew certainly whether or not the Lord Lovel would meet him; for, if he refused, he must take another method with him.

Lord Clifford was desirous to know the grounds of the quarrel; but Sir Philip declined entering into particulars at present, assuring him of a full information hereafter. He then sent M. Zadisky, attended by John Wyatt, and a servant of Lord Clifford, with a letter to Lord Lovel; the contents were as follows:

'My Lord Lovel!

'Sir Philip Harclay earnestly desires to see you at the house of Lord Clifford, where he waits to call you to account for the injuries done by you to the late Arthur Lord Lovel, your kinsman: If you accept his demand, he will make the Lord Clifford a witness and a judge of the cause; if not, he will expose you publicly as a traitor and a coward. Please to answer this letter, and he will acquaint you with the time, place, and manner of the meeting.

Philip Harclay.'

Zadisky presented the letter to Lord Lovel, informing him that he was the friend of Sir Philip Harclay. He seemed surprised and confounded at the contents; but, putting on an haughty air; I know nothing, said he, of the business this letter hints at: But wait a few hours, and I will give you an answer. He gave orders to treat Zadisky as a gentleman in every respect, except in avoiding his company; for the Greek had a shrewd and penetrating aspect, and he observed every turn of his countenance. The next day he came and apologized for his absence, and gave him the answer; sending his respects to the Lord Clifford. The messengers returned with all speed, and Sir Philip read the answer before all present.

'Lord Lovel knows not of any injuries done by him to the late Arthur Lord Lovel, whom he succeeded by just right of inheritance; nor of any right Sir Philip Harclay has, to call to account a man to whom he is barely known, having seen him only once, many years ago, at the house of his uncle, the old Lord Lovel: Nevertheless, Lord Lovel will not suffer any man to call his name and honour into question with impunity; for which reason he will meet Sir Philip Harclay at any time, place, and in what manner he shall appoint, bringing the same number of friends and dependants, that justice may be done to all parties.

Lovel.'

'Tis well, said Sir Philip: I am glad to find he has the spirit to meet me; he is an enemy worthy of my sword. Lord Clifford then proposed, that both parties should pass the borders, and obtain leave of the warden of the Scottish marches* to decide the quarrel in his jurisdiction, with a select number of friends on both sides. Sir Philip agreed to the proposal; and Lord Clifford wrote in his own name to ask permission of the Lord Graham, that his friends might come there; and obtained it, on condition that neither party should exceed a limited number of friends and followers.

Lord Clifford sent chosen messengers to Lord Lovel, acquainting him with the conditions and appointing the time, place, and manner of their meeting, and that he had been desired to accept the office of judge of the field. Lord Lovel accepted the conditions, and promised to be there without fail. Lord Clifford notified the same to Lord Graham, warden of the marches, who caused a piece of ground to be enclosed for the lists, and made preparations against the day appointed.

In the interim, Sir Philip Harclay thought proper to settle his worldly affairs: He made Zadisky acquainted with every circumstance of Edmund's history, and the obligation that lay upon him to revenge the death of his friend, and see justice done to his heir. Zadisky entered into the cause with an ardor that spoke the affection he bore to his friend. Why, said he, would you not suffer me to engage this traitor? Your life is of too much consequence to be staked against his: But tho' I trust that the justice of your cause must succeed, yet if it should happen otherwise, I vow to revenge you; he shall never go back from us both. However my hope and trust is, to see your arm the minister of justice. Sir Philip then sent for a lawyer and made his will, by which he appointed Edmund his chief heir by the name of Lovel, alias Seagrave, alias Twyford; he ordered that all his old friends, soldiers and servants, should be maintained in the same manner during their lives; he left to Zadisky an annuity of an hundred a year, and a legacy of two hundred pounds; one hundred pounds to a certain monastery; the same sum to be distributed among disbanded soldiers, and the same to the poor and needy in his neighbourhood.

He appointed Lord Clifford joint executor with Edmund, and gave his will into that nobleman's care, recommending Edmund to his favour and protection. If I live, said he, I will make him appear to be worthy of it; if I die, he will want a friend. I am desirous your Lordship, as a judge of the field, should be unprejudiced on either side, that you may judge impartially. If I die, Edmund's pretensions die with me; but my friend Zadisky will acquaint you with the foundation of them. I take these precautions because I ought to be prepared for every thing; but my heart is warm with better hopes, and I trust I shall live to justify my own cause, as well as that of my friend, who is a person of more consequence than he appears to be. Lord Clifford accepted the trust, and expressed the greatest reliance upon Sir Philip's honour and veracity.

While these preparations were making for the great event that was to decide the pretensions of Edmund, his enemies at the Castle of Lovel were brought to shame for their behaviour to him.

The disagreement between Wenlock and Markham had by degrees brought on an explanation of some parts of their conduct. Father Oswald had often hinted to the Baron, Wenlock's envy of Edmund's superior qualities, and the artifices by which he had obtained such an influence with Sir Robert, as to make him take his part upon all occasions. Oswald now took advantage of the breach between these two incendiaries, to persuade Markham to justify himself at Wenlock's expence, and to tell all he knew of his wickedness; at length he promised to declare all he knew of Wenlock's conduct, as well in France as since their return, when he should be called upon; and, by him, Oswald was enabled to unravel the whole of his contrivances, against the honour, interest, and even life of Edmund.

He prevailed on Hewson, and Kemp his associate, to add their testimony to the others. Hewson confessed that he was touched in his conscience, when he reflected on the cruelty and injustice of his behaviour to Edmund, whose behaviour towards him, after he had laid a snare for his life, was so noble and generous, that he was cut to the heart by it, and had suffered so much pain and remorse, that he longed for nothing so much as an opportunity to unburden his mind; but the dread of Mr. Wenlock's anger, and the effects of his resentment, had hitherto kept him silent, always hoping there would come a time when he might have leave to declare the whole truth.

Oswald conveyed this information to the Baron's ear, who waited for an opportunity to make the proper use of it. Not long after, the two principal incendiaries came to an open rupture, and Markham threatened Wenlock that he would shew his uncle what a serpent he had harboured in his bosom. The Baron arrested his words, and insisted upon his telling all he knew; adding, if you speak the truth I will support you, but if you prove false, I will punish you severely: As to Mr. Wenlock, he shall have a fair trial; and, if all the accusations I have heard are made good, it is high time that I should put him out of my family. The Baron, with a stern aspect, bade them follow him into the great hall; and sent for all the rest of the family together.

He then, with great solemnity, told them he was ready to hear all sides of the question. He declared the whole substance of his informations, and called upon the accusers to support the charge. Hewson and Kemp gave the same account they had done to Oswald, offering to swear to the truth of their testimony; several of the other servants related such circumstances as had come to their knowledge. Markham then spoke of every thing, and gave a particular account of all that had passed on the night they spent in the east apartment; he accursed himself of being privy to Wenlock's villany, called himself fool and blockhead for being the instrument of his malignant disposition, and asked pardon of his uncle for concealing it so long.

The Baron called upon Wenlock to reply to the charge; who, instead of answering, flew into a passion, raged, swore, threatened, and finally denied every thing. The witnesses persisted in their assertions. Markham desired leave to make known the reason why they were all afraid of him; he gives it out (said he), that he is to be my Lord's son-in-law; and they, supposing him to stand first in his favour, are afraid of his displeasure.—I hope, said the Baron, I shall not be at such a loss for a son-in-law, as to make choice of such a one as him; he never but once hinted at such a thing, and then I gave him no encouragement. I have long seen there was something very wrong in him; but I did not believe he was of so wicked a disposition: It is no wonder that princes should be so frequently deceived, when I, a private man, could be so much imposed upon within the circle of my own family. What think you, son Robert?—I, Sir, have been much more imposed on; and I take shame to myself on the occasion.—Enough, my son, said the Baron; a generous confession is only a proof of growing wisdom: You are now sensible, that the best of us are liable to imposition. The artifices of this unworthy kinsman have set us at variance with each other, and driven away an excellent youth from this house, to go I know not whither: But he shall no longer triumph in his wickedness; he shall feel what it is to be banished from the house of his protector. He shall set out for his mother's this very day; I will write to her in such a manner as shall inform her that he has offended me, without particularising the nature of his faults: I will give him an opportunity of recovering his credit with his own family, and this shall be my security against his doing further mischief. May he repent, and be forgiven!

Markham deserves punishment, but not in the same degree.— I confess it, said he, and will submit to whatever your Lordship shall enjoin.—You shall only be banished for a time, but he for ever. I will send you abroad on a business that shall put you in a way to do credit to yourself, and service to me. Son Robert, have you any objection to my sentence?—My Lord, said he, I have great reason to distrust myself; I am sensible of my own weakness, and your superior wisdom, as well as goodness, and I will henceforward submit to you in all things.

The Baron ordered two of his servants to pack up Wenlock's clothes and necessaries, and to set out with him that very day; he bade some others keep an eye upon him lest he should escape: As soon as they were ready, my Lord wished him a good journey, and gave him a letter for his mother. He departed without saying a word, in a sullen kind of resentment, but his countenance shewed the inward agitations of his mind.

As soon as he was gone every mouth was opened against him; a thousand stories came out that they never heard before: The Baron and his sons were astonished that he should go on so long without detection. My Lord sighed deeply at the thoughts of Edmund's expulsion, and ardently wished to know what was become of him.

Sir Robert took the opportunity of coming to an explanation with his brother William; he took shame to himself for some part of his past behaviour. Mr. William owned his affection to Edmund, and justified it by his merit and attachment to him, which were such that he was certain no time or distance could alter them. He accepted his brother's acknowledgement as a full amends for all that had past, and begged that henceforward an entire love and confidence might ever subsist between them.

These new regulations restored peace, confidence, and harmony, in the castle of Lovel.

At length the day arrived for the combatants to meet. The Lord Graham, with twelve followers gentlemen, and twelve servants, was ready at the dawn of day to receive them.

The first that entered the field was Sir Philip Harclay, Knight, armed compleatly, excepting his head-piece; Hugh Rugby, his Esquire, bearing his lance; John Barnard, his page, carrying his helmet and spurs; and two servants in his proper livery. The next came Edmund, the heir of Lovel, followed by his servant John Wyatt; Zadisky, followed by his servant.

At a short distance came the Lord Clifford, as judge of the field, with his Esquire, two pages, and two livery servants; followed by his eldest son, his nephew, and a gentleman his friend, each attended by one servant: He also brought a surgeon of note to take care of the wounded.

The Lord Graham saluted them; and, by his order, they took their places without the lists, and the trumpet sounded for the challenger. It was answered by the defendant, who soon after appeared, attended by three gentlemen his friends, with each one servant, beside his own proper attendants.

A place was erected for the Lord Clifford, as judge of the field; he desired Lord Graham would share the office, who accepted it on condition that the combatants should make no objection, and they agreed to it with the greatest courtesy and respect. They consulted together on many points of honour and ceremony between the two combatants.

They appointed a marshal of the field, and other inferior officers usually employed on these occasions. The Lord Graham sent the marshal for the challenger, desiring him to declare the cause of his quarrel before his enemy. Sir Philip Harclay then advanced, and thus spoke:

'I Philip Harclay, Knight, challenge Walter, commonly called Lord Lovel, as a base, treacherous and bloody man, who, by his wicked arts and devices, did kill, or cause to be killed, his kinsman, Arthur Lord Lovel, my dear and noble friend. I am called upon, in an extraordinary manner, to revenge his death; and I will prove the truth of what I have affirmed at the peril of my life.'

Lord Graham then bade the defendant answer to the charge. Lord Lovel stood forth before his followers, and thus replied:

'I Walter, Baron of Lovel, do deny the charge against me, and affirm it to be a base, false, and malicious accusation of this Sir Philip Harclay, which I believe to be invented by himself, or else framed by some enemy, and told to him for wicked ends; but be that as it may, I will maintain my own honour, and prove him to be a false traitor at the hazard of my own life, and to the punishment of his presumption.'

Then said the Lord Graham, will not this quarrel admit of arbitration?—No, replied Sir Philip; when I have justified this charge, I have more to bring against him. I trust in God and the justice of my cause, and defy that traitor to the death! Lord Clifford then spoke a few words to Lord Graham, who immediately called to the marshal and bade him open the lists, and deliver their weapons to the combatants.

While the marshal was arranging the combatants, and their followers, Edmund approached his friend and patron; he put one knee to the ground, he embraced his knees with the strongest emotions of grief and anxiety. He was dressed in compleat armour with his visor down; his device was a hawthorn, with a graft of the rose upon it, the motto— *This is not my true parent*;— but Sir Philip bade him take these words—*e fructu arbor cognoscitur.**

Sir Philip embraced the youth with strong marks of affection: Be composed, my child! said he; I have neither guilt, fear, nor doubt in me: I am so certain of success that I bid you be prepared for the consequence. Zadisky embraced his friend, he comforted Edmund, he suggested every thing that could confirm his hopes of success.

The marshal waited to deliver the spear to Sir Philip; he now presented it with the usual form.—Sir, receive your lance, and God defend the right!—Sir Philip answered, Amen! in a voice that was heard by all present.

He next presented his weapon to Lord Lovel with the same

sentence, who likewise answered Amen! with a good courage. Immediately the lists were cleared, and the combatants began the fight.

They contended a long time with equal skill and courage; at length Sir Philip unhorsed his antagonist. The judges ordered, that either he should alight, or suffer his enemy to remount; he chose the former, and a short combat on foot ensued. The sweat run off their bodies with the violence of the exercise. Sir Philip watched every motion of his enemy, and strove to weary him out, intending to wound but not to kill him, unless obliged for his own safety.

He thrust his sword through his left arm, and demanded whether he would confess the fact? Lord Lovel enraged, answered, he would die sooner. Sir Philip then passed the sword through his body twice, and Lord Lovel fell, crying out that he was slain.

I hope not, said Sir Philip, for I have a great deal of business for you to do before you die: Confess your sins, and endeavour to atone for them, as the only ground to hope for pardon.—Lord Lovel replied, You are the victor, use your good fortune generously!

Sir Philip took away his sword, and then waved it over his head, and beckoned for assistance. The judges sent to beg Sir Philip to spare the life of his enemy. I will, said he, upon condition that he will make an honest confession.

Lord Lovel desired a surgeon and a confessor. You shall have both, said Sir Philip; but you must first answer me a question or two. Did you kill your kinsman or not?—It was not my hand that killed him, answered the wounded man.—It was done by your own order, however? You shall have no assistance till you answer this point.—It was, said he, and Heaven is just!—Bear witness all present, said Sir Philip; he confesses the fact!

He then beckoned Edmund, who approached.—Take off your helmet, said he: Look on that youth, he is the son of your injured kinsman.—It is himself! said the Lord Lovel, and fainted away.

Sir Philip then called for a surgeon and a priest, both of which Lord Graham had provided; the former began to bind up his wounds and his assistants poured a cordial into his mouth. Preserve his life, if it be possible, said Sir Philip; for much depends upon it.

He then took Edmund by the hand, and presented him to all the company. In this young man, said he, you see the true heir of the house of Lovel! Heaven has in its own way made him the instrument to discover the death of his parents. His father was assassinated by order of that wicked man, who now receives his punishment; his mother was, by his cruel treatment, compelled to leave her own house; she was delivered in the fields, and perished herself in seeking a shelter for her infant. I have sufficient proofs of every thing I say, which I am ready to communicate to every person who desires to know the particulars: Heaven, by my hand, has chastised him; he has confessed the fact I accuse him of, and it remains that he make restitution of the fortune and honours he hath usurped so long.

Edmund kneeled, and with uplifted hands returned thanks to Heaven, that his noble friend and champion was crowned with victory!—The Lords and gentlemen gathered round them, they congratulated them both; while Lord Lovel's friends and followers were employed in taking care of him. Lord Clifford took Sir Philip's hand.—You have acted with so much honour and prudence that it is presumptuous to offer you advice; but what mean you to do with the wounded man?—I have not determined, said he; I thank you for the hint, and beg your advice how to proceed.—Let us consult Lord Graham, replied he.—Lord Graham insisted upon their going all to his castle; there, said he, you will have impartial witnesses of all that passes. Sir Philip was unwilling to give so much trouble. The Lord Graham protested he should be proud to do any service to so noble a gentleman. Lord Clifford enforced his request, saying, it was better upon all accounts to keep their prisoner on this side the borders till they saw what turn his health would take, and to keep him safely till he had settled his worldly affairs.

This resolution being taken, Lord Graham invited the wounded man and his friends to his castle, as being the nearest place where he could be lodged and taken proper care of, it being dangerous to carry him further. They accepted the proposal with many acknowledgements; and, having made a kind of litter of boughs, they all proceeded to Lord Graham's castle, where they put Lord Lovel to bed, and the surgeon dressed his wounds, and desired he might be kept quiet, not knowing at present whether they were dangerous or not.

About an hour after, the wounded man complained of thirst; he asked for the surgeon, and enquired if his life was in danger? The surgeon answered him doubtfully. He asked, where is Sir Philip Harclay?—In the castle.—Where is that young man whom he calls the heir of Lovel?—He is here, too.—Then I am surrounded with my enemies. I want to speak to one of my own servants, without witnesses; let one be sent to me.

The surgeon withdrew, and acquainted the gentlemen below. He shall not speak to any man, said Sir Philip, but in my presence. He went with him into the sick man's room. Upon the sight of Sir Philip, he seemed in great agitation.—Am I not allowed to speak with my own servant, said he?—Yes, Sir, you may; but not without witnesses.—Then I am a prisoner, it seems?—No, not so Sir; but some caution is necessary at present: But compose yourself, I do not wish for your death.—Then why did you seek it? I never injured you.—Yes, you have, in the person of my friend, and I am only the instrument of justice in the hand of Heaven; endeavour to make atonement while life is spared to you.—Shall I send the priest to you? perhaps he may convince you of the necessity of restitution, in order to obtain forgiveness of your sins.

Sir Philip sent for the priest and the surgeon, and obliged the servant to retire with him. I leave you, Sir, to the care of these gentlemen; and whenever a third person is admitted, I will be his attendant: I will visit you again within an hour. He then retired, and consulted his friends below; they were of opinion that no time should be lost. You will then, said he, accompany me into the sick man's apartment in an hour's time.

Within the hour, Sir Philip, attended by Lord Clifford and Lord Graham, entered the chamber. Lord Lovel was in great emotion; the priest stood on one side of the bed, the surgeon on the other; the former exhorted him to confess his sins, the other desired he might be left to his repose. Lord Lovel seemed in great anguish of mind; he trembled, and was in the utmost confusion. Sir Philip intreated him, with the piety of a confessor, to consider his soul's health before that of his body. He then asked Sir Philip, by what means he knew that he was concerned in the death of his kinsman?—Sir, replied he, it was not merely by human means this fact was discovered. There is a certain apartment in the castle of Lovel, that has been shut up these one and twenty years,* but has lately been opened and examined into.

Oh Heaven! exclaimed he, then Geoffry must have betrayed me!—No, Sir, he has not, it was revealed in a very extraordinary manner to that youth whom it most concerns.—How can he be the heir of Lovel?—By being the son of that unfortunate woman, whom you cruelly obliged to leave her own house, to avoid being compelled to wed the murderer of her husband: We are not ignorant, moreover, of the fictitious funeral you made for her. All is discovered, and you will not tell us any more than we know already; but we desire to have it confirmed by your confession.—The judgments of Heaven are fallen upon me! said Lord Lovel. I am childless, and one is arisen from the grave to claim my inheritance.—Nothing then hinders you to do justice and make restitution; it is for the ease of your conscience; and you have no other way of making atonement for all the mischief you have done.—You know too much, said the criminal, and I will relate what you do not know.

You may remember, proceeded he, that I saw you once at my uncle's house?—I well remember it.—At that time my mind was disturbed by the baleful passion of envy; it was from that root all my bad actions sprung.—Praise be to God! said the good priest; he hath touched your heart with true contrition, and you shew the effect of his mercies; you will do justice, and you will be rewarded by the gift of repentance unto salvation.—Sir Philip desired the penitent to proceed.

My kinsman excelled me in every kind of merit, in the graces of person and mind, in all his exercises, and in every accomplishment. I was totally eclipsed by him, and I hated to be in his company; but what finished my aversion, was his addressing the lady upon whom I had fixed my affections: I strove to rival him there, but she gave him the preference that, indeed, was only his due; but I could not bear to see, or acknowledge, it.

The most bitter hatred took possession of my breast, and I vowed to revenge the supposed injury as soon as opportunity should offer. I buried my resentment deep in my heart, and outwardly appeared to rejoice at his success; I made a merit of resigning my pretensions to him, but I could not bear to be present at his nuptials: I retired to my father's seat, and brooded over my revenge in secret. My father died this year, and soon after my uncle followed him; within another year my kinsman was summoned to attend the King on his Welch expedition.

As soon as I heard he was gone from home, I resolved to prevent his return, exulting in the prospect of possessing his title, fortune, and his Lady. I hired messengers, who were constantly going and coming to give me intelligence of all that passed at the castle; I went there soon after, under pretence of visiting my kinsman. My spies brought me an account of all that happened; one informed me of the event of the battle, but could not tell whether my rival was living or dead; I hoped the latter, that I might avoid the crime I mediated: I reported his death to his Lady, who took it very heavily.

Soon after a messenger arrived with tidings that he was alive and well, and had obtained leave to return home immediately.

I instantly dispatched my two emissaries to intercept him on the way. He made so much haste to return, that he was met within a mile of his own castle: he had out-rode his servants and was alone: They killed him, and drew him aside out of the highway. They then came to me with all speed, and desired my orders; it was then about sunset: I sent them back to fetch the dead body, which they brought privately into the castle: They tied it neck and heels, and put it into a trunk, which they buried under the floor in the closet you mentioned. The sight of the body stung me to the heart; I then felt the pangs of remorse, but it was too late: I took every precaution that prudence suggested to prevent the discovery; but nothing can be concealed from the eye of Heaven.

From that fatal hour I have never known peace, always in fear of something impending to discover my guilt, and to bring me to shame: At length I am overtaken by justice. I am brought to a severe reckoning here, and I dread to meet one more severe hereafter.

Enough, said the priest, you have done a good work, my son! trust in the Lord, and, now this burden is off your mind, the rest will be made easy to you.

Lord Lovel took a minute's repose, and then went on.—I hope by the hint you gave, Sir Philip, the poor lady is yet alive?—No, Sir, she is not; but she died not till after she brought forth a son, whom Heaven made its instrument to discover and avenge the death of both his parents.—They are well avenged! said he. I have no children to lament for me, all mine have been taken from me in the bloom of youth; only one daughter lived to be twelve years old; I intended her for a wife for one of my nephews, but within three months I have buried her. He sighed, wept, and was silent.

The gentlemen present lifted up their hands and eyes to Heaven in silence. The will of Heaven be obeyed! said the priest. My penitent hath confessed all; what more would you require?— That he make atonement, said Sir Philip; that he surrender the title and estate to the right heir, and dispose of his own proper fortune to his nearest relations, and resign himself to penitence and preparation for a future state. For this time I leave him with you, Father, and will join my prayers with yours for his repentance.

So saying, he left the room, and was followed by the Barons and the surgeon; the priest alone remaining with him. As soon as they were out of hearing, Sir Philip questioned the surgeon concerning his patient's situation; who answered, that at present he saw no signs of immediate danger, but he could not yet pronounce that there was none: if he were mortally wounded, said he, he could not be so well, nor speak so long without faintness; and it is my opinion that he will soon recover, if nothing happens to retard the cure.—Then, said Sir Philip, keep this opinion from him; for I would suffer the fear of death to operate on him until he hath performed some necessary acts of justice: Let it only be known to these noblemen, upon whose honour I can rely, and I trust they will approve my request to you, Sir.—I join in it, said Lord Clifford, from the same motives.—I insist upon it, said Lord Graham; and I can answer for my surgeon's discretion.— My Lords, said the surgeon, you may depend on my fidelity; and, after what I have just heard, my conscience is engaged in this noble gentleman's behalf, and I will do every thing in my power to second your intentions.—I thank you, Sir, said Sir Philip, and you may depend on my gratitude in return. I presume you will sit up with him to-night; if any danger should arise, I desire to be called immediately; but, otherwise, I would suffer him to rest quietly, that he may be prepared for the business of the following day.—I shall obey your directions, Sir; my necessary attendance will give me a pretence not to leave him, and thus I shall hear all that passes between him and all that visit him.—You will oblige me highly, said Sir Philip, and I shall go to rest with confidence in your care.

The surgeon returned to the sick man's chamber, Sir Philip and the Barons to the company below: They supped in the great hall with all the gentlemen that were present at the combat. Sir Philip and his Edmund retired to their repose, being heartily fatigued; and the company staid to a late hour, commenting upon the action of the day, praising the courage and generosity of the noble Knight, and wishing a good event to his undertaking.

Most of Lord Lovel's friends went away as soon as they saw him safely lodged, being ashamed of him, and of their appearance in his behalf; and the few that stayed were induced by their desire of a further information of the base action he had committed, and to justify their own characters and conduct.

The next morning Sir Philip entered into consultation with the two Barons, on the methods he should take to get Edmund received, and acknowledged, as heir of the house of Lovel. They were all of opinion, that the criminal should be kept in fear till he had settled his worldly affairs, and they had resolved how to dispose of him. With this determination they entered his room, and enquired of the surgeon how he had passed the night? He shook his head, and said but little.

Lord Lovel desired that he might be removed to his own

house. Lord Graham said, he could not consent to that, as there was evident danger in removing him; and appealed to the surgeon, who confirmed his opinion. Lord Graham desired he would make himself easy, and that he should have every kind of assistance there.

Sir Philip then proposed to send for the Lord Fitz-Owen, who would see that all possible care was taken of his brother-in-law, and would assist him in settling his affairs. Lord Lovel was against it; he was peevish and uneasy, and desired to be left with only his own servants to attend him. Sir Philip quitted the room with a significant look; and the two Lords endeavoured to reconcile him to his situation. He interrupted them. — It is easy for men in your situation to advise, but it is difficult for one in mine to practise; wounded in body and mind, it is natural that I should strive to avoid the extremes of shame and punishment: I thank you for your kind offices, and beg I may be left with my own servants. — With them, and the surgeon, you shall, said Lord Graham; and they both retired.

Sir Philip met them below. My Lords, said he, I am desirous that my Lord Fitz-Owen should be sent for, and that he may hear his brother's confession; for I suspect that he may hereafter deny, what only the fear of death has extorted from him: With your permission I am determined to send messengers to-day. They both expressed approbation, and Lord Clifford proposed to write to him, saying, a letter from an impartial person will have the more weight: I will send one of my principal domesticks with your own. This measure being resolved upon, Lord Clifford retired to write, and Sir Philip to prepare his servants for instant departure. Edmund desired leave to write to Father Oswald, and John Wyatt was ordered to be the bearer of his letter. When the Lord Clifford had finished his letter, he read it to Sir Philip and his chosen friends, as follows:

'Right Hon. my good Lord,

'I have taken upon me to acquaint your Lordship, that there has been a solemn combat at arms between your brother-in-law, the Lord Lovel, and Sir Philip Harclay, Knt. of Yorkshire. It was fought in the jurisdiction of the Lord Graham, who with myself, was appointed judge of the field; it was fairly won, and Sir Philip is the conqueror. After he had gained the victory he declared at large the cause of the quarrel, and that he had revenged the death of Arthur Lord Lovel his friend, whom the present Lord Lovel had assassinated, that he might enjoy his title and estate. The wounded man confessed the fact: and Sir Philip gave him his life, and only carried off his sword as a trophy of his victory. Both the victor and the vanquished were conveyed to Lord Graham's castle, where the Lord Lovel now lies in great danger. He is desirous to settle his worldly affairs, and to make his peace with God and man. Sir Philip Harclay says, there is a male heir of the house of Lovel, for whom he claims the title and estate; but he is very desirous that your Lordship should be present at the disposal of your brother's property that of right belongs to him, of which your children are the undoubted heirs: He also wants to consult you in many other points of honour and equity. Let me intreat you, on the receipt of this letter, to set out immediately for Lord Graham's castle, where you will be received with the utmost respect and hospitality. You will hear things that will surprise you as much as they do me; you will judge of them with that justice and honour that speaks your character; and you will unite with us in wondering at the ways of providence, and submitting to its decrees, in punishing the guilty, and doing justice to the innocent and oppressed. My best wishes and prayers attend you and your hopeful family. My Lord, I remain your humble servant.

Clifford.'

Every one present expressed the highest approbation of this letter. Sir Philip gave orders to John Wyatt to be very circumspect in his behaviour, to give Edmund's letter privately to Father Oswald, and to make no mention of him, or his pretensions to Lovel castle.

Lord Clifford gave his servant the requisite precautions. Lord Graham added a note of invitation, and sent it by a servant of his own.—As soon as all things were ready, the messengers set out with all speed for the Castle of Lovel.

They staid no longer by the way than to take some refreshment, but rode night and day till they arrived there.

Lord Fitz-Owen was in the parlour with his children. Father Oswald was walking in the avenue before the house, when he saw three messengers whose horses seemed jaded and the riders fatigued, like men come a long journey. He came up, just as the first had delivered his message to the porter. John Wyatt knew him, he dismounted, and made signs that he had something to say to him; he retired back a few steps, and John, with great dexterity, slipped a letter into his hand. The Father gave him his blessing, and a welcome. Who do you come from? said he aloud.—From the Lords Graham and Clifford to the Lord Fitz-Owen; and we bring letters of consequence to the Baron.

Oswald followed the messengers into the hall, a servant announced their arrival. Lord Fitz-Owen received them in the parlour: Lord Clifford's servant delivered his master's letter, Lord Graham's his, and they said they would retire and wait his Lordship's answer. The Baron ordered them some refreshment. They retired, and he opened his letters: He read them with great agitations, he struck his hand upon his heart, he exclaimed—My fears are all verified! the blow is struck, and it has fallen upon the guilty!

Oswald came in a minute after. You are come in good time, said the Baron. Read that letter, that my children may know the contents. He read it, with faultering voice, and trembling limbs. They were all in great surprise. William looked down, and kept a studied silence. Sir Robert exclaimed—Is it possible? can my Uncle be guilty of such an action?—You hear, said the Baron, he has confessed it!—But to whom? said Sir Robert.—His father replied, Lord Clifford's honour is unquestionable, and I cannot doubt what he affirms.

Sir Robert leaned his head upon his hand, as one lost in thought: At length he seemed to awake—My Lord, I have no doubt that Edmund is at the bottom of this business. Do you not remember, that Sir Philip Harclay long ago promised him his friendship? Edmund disappears; and, soon after, this man challenges my Uncle. You know what passed here before his departure: He has suggested this affair to Sir Philip, and instigated him to this action. This is the return he has made for the favours he has received from our family, to which he owes every thing.—Softly, my son! said the Baron; let us be cautious of reflecting upon Edmund: There is a greater hand in this business. My conjecture was too true: It was in that fatal apartment that he was made acquainted with the circumstances of Lord Lovel's death; he was, perhaps, enjoined to reveal them to Sir Philip Harclay, the bosom friend of the deceased. The mystery of that apartment is disclosed, the woe to the guilty is accomplished! There is no reflection upon any one; Heaven effects its purposes in its own time and manner. I and mine are innocent; let us worship, and be silent!

But what do you propose to do? said Sir Robert.—To return with the messengers, answered the Baron. I think it highly proper that I should see your Uncle, and hear what he has to say: My children are his heirs; in justice to them I ought to be acquainted with every thing that concerns the disposal of his fortune. Your Lordship is in the right, answered Sir Robert, it concerns us all. I have only to ask your permission to bear you company.—With all my heart, said the Baron: I have only to ask of you in return, that you will command yourself, and not speak your mind hastily; wait for the proofs before you give judgment, and take advice of your reason before you decide upon any thing: If you reflect upon the past, you will find reason to distrust yourself. Leave all to me, and be assured I will protect your honour and my own.—I will obey you in all things, my Lord; and will make immediate preparation for our departure. So saying, he left the room.

As soon as he was gone, Mr. William broke silence. My Lord, said he, if you have no great objection, I beg leave also to accompany you both.—You shall, my son, if you desire it; I think I can see your motives, and your brother's also; your coolness will be a good balance to his warmth: You shall go with us. My son Walter shall be his sister's protector in our absence, and he shall be master here till we return.—I hope, my dear father, that will not be long; I shall not be happy till you come home, said the fair Emma.—It shall be no longer, my dearest, than till this untoward affair is settled. The Baron desired to know when the messengers were expected to return. Oswald took this opportunity to retire; he went to his own apartment, and read the letter, as follows:

'The Heir of Lovel, to his dear and reverend friend, Father Oswald.

'Let my friends at the Castle of Lovel know that I live in hopes one day to see them there. If you could by any means return with the messengers, your testimony would add weight to mine; perhaps you might obtain permission to attend the Baron: I leave it to you to manage this. John Wyatt will inform you of all that has passed here, and that hitherto my success has outran my expectation, and, almost, my wishes. I am in the high road to my inheritance; and trust that the Power who hath conducted me thus far, will not leave his work unfinished. Tell my beloved William that I live, and hope to embrace him before long. I recommend myself to your holy prayers and blessing, and remain your son and servant,

Edmund.'

Oswald then went to the messengers; he drew John Wyatt to a distance from the rest, and got the information he wanted: He stayed with him till he was sent for by the Baron, to whom he went directly, and prevented his questions, by saying, I have been talking with the messengers: I find they have travelled night and day to bring the letters with all speed; they only require one night's rest, and will be ready to set out with you to-morrow.—'Tis well, said the Baron; we will set out as soon as they are ready.—My Lord, said Oswald, I have a favour to beg of you; it is that I may attend you: I have seen the progress of this wonderful discovery, and I have a great desire to see the conclusion of it; perhaps my presence may be of service in the course of your business.—Perhaps it may, said the Baron; I have no objection, if you desire to go.—They then separated, and went to prepare for their journey.

Oswald had a private interview with Joseph, whom he informed of all that he knew, and his resolution to attend the

Baron in his journey to the north. I go, said he, to bear witness in behalf of injured innocence: If it be needful, I shall call upon you; therefore, hold yourself in readiness in case you should be sent for.—That I will, said Joseph, and spend my last remains of life and strength, to help my young Lord to his right and title; but do they not begin to suspect who is the Heir of Lovel?—Not in the least, said Oswald; they think him concerned in the discovery, but have no idea of his being interested in the event.—Oh Father, said Joseph, I shall think every day a week till your return; but I will no longer keep you from your repose.—Good night, said Oswald; but I have another visit to pay before I go to rest.

He left Joseph, and went on tip-toe to Mr. William's room and tapped at his door; he came and opened it. What news, Father?— Not much; I have only orders to tell you that Edmund is well, and as much your friend as ever.—I guessed, said William, that we should hear something of him: I have still another guess.—What is that, my child?—That we shall see or hear of him where we are going.—It is very likely, said Oswald; and I would have you be prepared for it: I am confident we shall hear nothing to his discredit.—I am certain of that, said William, and I shall rejoice to see him: I conclude that he is under the protection of Sir Philip Harclay.—He is so, said Oswald; I had my information from Sir Philip's servant, who is one of the messengers, and was guide to the others in their way hither. After some farther conversation they separated, and each went to his repose.

The next morning the whole party set out on their journey; they travelled by easy stages on account of the Baron's health, which began to be impaired, and arrived in health and spirits at the Castle of Lord Graham, where they were received with the utmost respect and kindness by the noble Master.

The Lord Lovel had recovered his health and strength as much as possible in the time, and was impatient to be gone from thence to his own house. He was surprised to hear of the arrival of his brother and nephews, and expressed no pleasure at the thoughts of seeing them. When Sir Philip Harclay came to pay his respects to Baron Fitz-Owen, the latter received him with civility, but with a coldness that was apparent. Sir Robert left the room, doubting his resolution. Sir Philip advanced, and took the Baron by the hand. My Lord, said he, I rejoice to see you here! I cannot be satisfied with the bare civilities of such a man as you. I aspire to your esteem, to your friendship, and I shall not be happy till I obtain them. I will make you the judge of every part of my conduct, and where you shall condemn me, I will condemn myself.

The Baron was softened, his noble heart felt its alliance with its counterpart, but he thought the situation of his brother demanded some reserve towards the man who sought his life; but, in spite of himself, it wore off every moment. Lord Clifford related all that had passed, with the due regard to Sir Philip's honour; he remarked how nobly he concealed the cause of his resentment against the Lord Lovel till the day of combat, that he might not prepossess the judges against him. He enlarged on his humanity to the vanquished, on the desire he expressed to have justice done to his heirs; finally, he mentioned his great respect for the Lord Fitz-Owen, and the solicitude he shewed to have him come to settle the estate of the sick man in favour of his children. Lord Clifford also employed his son to soften Sir Robert, and to explain to him every doubtful part of Sir Philip's behaviour.

After the travellers had taken some rest, the Lord Graham proposed that they should make a visit to the sick man's chamber. The Lords sent to acquaint him they were coming to visit him, and they followed the messenger. The Lord Fitz-Owen went up to the bedside; he embraced his brother with strong emotions of concern. Sir Robert followed him; then Mr. William. Lord Lovel embraced them, but said nothing; his countenance shewed his inward agitations.—Lord Fitz-Owen first broke silence. I hope, said he, I see my brother better than I expected? Lord Lovel bit his fingers, he pulled the bed clothes, he seemed almost distracted; at length he broke out—I owe no thanks to those who sent for my relations! Sir Philip Harclay, you have used ungenerously the advantage you have gained over me! you spared my life only to take away my reputation. You have exposed me to strangers, and, what is worse, to my dearest friends; when I lay in a state of danger, you obliged me to say any thing, and now you take advantage of it, to ruin me in my friends affection: But, if I recover, you may repent it!

Sir Philip then came forward. My Lords, I shall take no notice of what this unhappy man has just now said; I shall appeal to you, as to the honourable witnesses of all that has passed: You see it was no more than necessary. I appeal to you for the motives of my treatment of him, before, at, and after our meeting. I did not take his life as I might have done; I wished him to repent of his sins, and to make restitution of what he unjustly possesses. I was called out to do an act of justice; I had taken the heir of Lovel under my protection, my chief view was to see justice done to him; what regarded this man was but a secondary motive. This was my end, and I will never, never lose sight of it.

Lord Lovel seemed almost choaked with passion, to see every one giving some mark of approbation and respect to Sir Philip. He called out, I demand to know who is this pretended heir whom he brings out to claim my title and fortune?—My noble auditors, said Sir Philip, I shall appeal to your judgment in regard to the proofs of my ward's birth and family! every circumstance shall be laid before you, and you shall decide upon them.

Here is a young man, supposed the son of a peasant, who by a train of circumstances that could not have happened by human contrivance, discovers not only who are his real parents, but that they came to untimely deaths. He even discovers the different places where their bones are buried, both out of consecrated ground, and appeals to their ashes for the truth of his pretensions. He has also living proofs to offer, that will convince the most incredulous. I have deferred entering into particulars till the arrival of Baron Fitz-Owen; I know his noble heart and honourable character, from one that has long been an eye-witness of his goodness; such is the opinion I have of his justice, that I will accept him as one of the judges in his brother's cause: I and my ward will bring our proofs before him, and the company here present; in the course of them it will appear that he is the best qualified of any to judge of them, because he can ascertain many of the facts we shall have occasion to mention: I will rest our cause upon their decision.

Lord Graham applauded Sir Philip's appeal, affirming his own impartiality, and calling upon Lord Clifford and his son, and also his own nephews who were present. Lord Clifford said, Sir Philip offers fairly, and like himself; there can be no place nor persons more impartial than the present, and I presume the Lord Lovel can have no objection.—No objection! answered he; what, to be tried like a criminal, to have judges appointed over me to decide upon my right to my own estate and title? I will not submit to such a jurisdiction!—Then, said Sir Philip, you had rather be tried by the laws of the land, and have them pronounce sentence upon you? Take your choice, Sir; if you refuse the one, you shall be certain of the other. Lord Clifford then said, you will allow Lord Lovel to consider of the proposal; he will consult his friends, and be determined by their advice.—Lord Fitz-Owen said, I am very much surprised at what I have heard. I should be glad to know all that Sir Philip Harclay has to say for his ward, that I may judge what my brother has to hope or fear; I will then give my best advice, or offer my mediation as he may stand in need of them.—You say well, replied Lord Graham; and pray let us come directly to the point: Sir Philip, you will introduce your ward to this company, and enter upon your proofs.

Sir Philip bowed to the company, he went out and brought in Edmund, encouraging him by the way; he presented him to Baron Fitz-Owen, who looked very serious. Edmund Twyford, said he, are you the heir of the house of Lovel?—I am, my Lord, said Edmund, bowing to the ground; the proofs will appear; but I am, at the same time, the most humble and grateful of all your servants, and the servant of your virtues. Sir Robert rose up, and was going to leave the room. Son Robert, stay, said the Baron: If there is any fraud you will be pleased to detect it, and if all that is affirmed be true, you will not shut your eyes against the light; you are concerned in this business, hear it in silence, and let reason be arbiter in your cause. He bowed to his father, bit his lip, and retired to the window. William nodded to Edmund, and was silent. All the company had their eyes fixed on the young man, who stood in the midst, casting down his eyes with modest respect to the audience; while Sir Philip related all the material circumstances of his life, the wonderful gradation by which he came to the knowledge of his birth, the adventures of the haunted apartment, the discovery of the fatal closet, and the presumptive proofs that Lord Lovel was buried there. At this part of his narration, Lord Fitz-Owen interrupted him—Where is this closet you talk of, for I and my sons went over the apartment since Edmund's departure, and found no such place, as you describe?—My Lord, said Edmund, I can account for it; the door is covered with tapestry, the same as the room, and you might easily overlook it; but I have a witness here, said he, and putting his hand into his bosom, he drew out the key. If this is not the key of that closet, let me be deemed an impostor, and all I say a falsehood; I will risk my pretensions upon this proof.

And for what purpose did you take it away? said the Baron.— To prevent any person from going into it, replied Edmund; I have vowed to keep it till I shall open that closet before witnesses appointed for that purpose.—Proceed, Sir, said the Baron Fitz-Owen.—Sir Philip then related the conversation between Edmund and Margery Twyford, his supposed mother.—Lord Fitz-Owen seemed in the utmost surprise: He exclaimed, can this be true? strange discovery! unfortunate child!—Edmund's tears bore witness to his veracity; he was obliged to hide his face, he lifted up his clasped hands to Heaven, and was in great emotions during all this part of the relation; while Lord Lovel groaned, and seemed in great agitation.

Sir Philip then addressed himself to Lord Fitz-Owen. My Lord, there was another person present at the conversation between Edmund and his foster-mother, who can witness to all that passed; perhaps your Lordship can tell who that was?—It was Father Oswald, replied the Baron; I will remember that he went with him at his request; let him be called in. He was sent for, and came immediately. The Baron desired him to relate all that passed between Edmund and his mother.

Oswald then began.—Since I am now properly called upon to testify what I know concerning this young man, I will speak the truth without fear or favour of any one; and I will swear by the rules of my holy order, to the truth of what I shall relate. He then gave a particular account of all that passed on that occasion, and mentioned the tokens found on both the infant and his mother. Where are these tokens to be seen, said the Lord Clifford?—I have them here, my Lord, said Edmund, and I keep them as my greatest treasures. He then produced them before all the company. There is no appearance of any fraud or collusion, said Lord Graham; if any man thinks he sees any, let him speak.—Pray, my Lord, suffer me to speak a word, said Sir Robert. Do you remember that I hinted my suspicions concerning Father Oswald, the night our kinsmen lay in the east apartment?—I do, said the Baron.—Well, Sir, it now appears that he did know more than he would tell us; you find he is very deep in all Edmund's secrets, and you may judge what were his motives for undertaking this journey.—I observe what you say, answered his father, but let us hear all that Oswald has to say: I will be as impartial as possible. My Lord, returned Oswald, I beg you also to recollect what I said on the night your son speaks of, concerning secrecy in certain matters.—I remember that also, said the Baron; but proceed. My Lord, continued Oswald, I knew more than I thought myself at liberty to disclose at that time; but I will now tell you every thing. I saw there was something more than common in the accidents that befel this young man, and in his being called out to sleep in the east apartment; I earnestly desired him to let me be with him on the second night, to which he consented reluctantly; we heard a great noise in the rooms underneath, we went down stairs together, I saw him open the fatal closet, I heard groans that pierced me to the heart, I kneeled down and prayed for the repose of the spirit departed; I found a seal with the arms of Lovel engraven upon it, which I gave to Edmund, and he now has it in his possession: He enjoined me to keep secret what I had seen and heard, till the time should come to declare it. I conceived that I was called to be a witness of these things; besides my curiosity was excited to know the event; I, therefore, desired to be present at the interview between him and his mother, which was affecting beyond expression: I heard what I have now declared as nearly as my memory permits me. I hope no impartial person will blame me for any part of my conduct; but if they should, I do not repent it: If I should forfeit the favour of the rich and great, I shall have acquitted myself to God and my conscience. I have no worldly ends to answer; I plead the cause of the injured orphan; and I think also that I second the designs of providence.—You have well spoken, Father, said the Lord Clifford; your testimony is indeed of consequence.

It is amazing and convincing, said Lord Graham; and the whole story is so well connected, that I can see nothing to make us doubt the truth of it: But let us examine the proofs. Edmund gave into their hands the necklace and ear-rings; he shewed them the locket with the cypher of Lovel, and the seal with the arms; he told them the cloak in which he was wrapped was in the custody of his foster-mother, who would produce it on demand. He begged that some proper persons might be commissioned to go with him to examine whether or no the bodies of his parents were buried where he affirmed; adding, that he put his pretensions into their hands with pleasure, relying entirely upon their honour and justice.

During this interesting scene, the criminal covered his face, and was silent; but he sent forth bitter sighs and groans that denoted the anguish of his heart. At length, Lord Graham, in compassion to him, proposed that they should retire and consider of the proofs; adding, Lord Lovel must needs be fatigued; we will resume the subject in his presence, when he is disposed to receive us. Sir Philip Harclay approached the bed: Sir, said he, I now leave you in the hands of your own relations; they are men of strict honour, and I confide in them to take care of you and of your concern. They then went out of the room, leaving only the Lord Fitz-Owen and his sons with the criminal. They discoursed of the wonderful story of Edmund's birth, and the principal events of his life.

After dinner Sir Philip requested another conference with the Lords, and their principal friends. There was present also, Father Oswald and Lord Graham's confessor, who had taken the Lord Lovel's confession, Edmund and Zadisky. Now gentlemen, said

Sir Philip, I desire to know your opinion of our proofs, and your advice upon them.

Lord Graham replied, I am desired to speak for the rest: We think there are strong presumptive proofs that this young man is the true heir of Lovel; but they ought to be confirmed and authenticated. Of the murder of the late Lord there is no doubt; the criminal hath confessed it, and the circumstances confirm it; the proofs of his crime are so connected with those of the young man's birth, that one cannot be public without the other. We are desirous to do justice, and yet are unwilling, for the Lord Fitz-Owen's sake, to bring the criminal to public shame and punishment. We wish to find out a medium; we therefore desire Sir Philip to make proposals for his ward, and let Lord Fitz-Owen answer for himself and his brother, and we will be moderators between them. Here every one expressed approbation, and called upon Sir Philip to make his demands.

If, said he, I were to demand strict justice, I should not be satisfied with any thing less than the life of the criminal; but I am a christian soldier, the disciple of him who came into the world to save sinners; for his sake, continued he (crossing himself), I forego my revenge, I spare the guilty: If Heaven gives him time for repentance, man should not deny it. It is my ward's particular request, that I will not bring shame upon the house of his benefactor, the Lord Fitz-Owen, for whom he hath a filial affection and profound veneration. My proposals are these; first, that the criminal make restitution of the title and estate obtained with so much injustice and cruelty to the lawful heir, whom he shall acknowledge such before proper witnesses. Secondly, that he shall surrender his own lawful inheritance and personal estate into the hands of the Lord Fitz-Owen, in trust for his sons, who are his heirs of blood. Thirdly, that he shall retire into a religious house, or else quit the kingdom in three months time; and, in either case, those who enjoy his fortune shall allow him a decent annuity, that he may not want the comforts of life. By the last I disable him from the means of doing further mischief, and enable him to devote the remainder of his days to penitence. These are my proposals, and I give him four and twenty hours to consider of them; if he refuses to comply with them, I shall be obliged to proceed to severer measures, and to a public prosecution: But the goodness of the Lord Fitz-Owen bids me expect, from his influence with his brother, a compliance with proposals, made out of respect to his honourable character.

Lord Graham applauded the humanity, prudence, and piety of Sir Philip's proposals. He enforced them with all his influence and eloquence. Lord Clifford seconded him; and the rest gave tokens of approbation. Sir Robert Fitz-Owen then rose up—I beg leave to observe to the company, who are going to dispose so generously of another man's property, that my father purchased the castle and estate of the house of Lovel; who is to repay him the money for it?

Sir Philip then said, I have also a question to ask. Who is to pay the arrears of my ward's estate, which he has unjustly been kept out of these one and twenty years? Let Lord Clifford answer to both points, for he is not interested in either?—Lord Clifford smiled.—I think, returned he, the first question is answered by the second, and that the parties concerned should set one against the other, especially as Lord Fitz-Owen's children will inherit the fortune, which includes the purchase-money. Lord Graham said, this determination is both equitable and generous, and I hope will answer the expectations on all sides.—I have another proposal to make to my Lord Fitz-Owen, said Sir Philip; but I first wait for the acceptance of those already made.—Lord Fitz-Owen replied, I shall report them to my brother, and acquaint the company with his resolution to-morrow.

They then separated; and the Baron, with his sons, returned to the sick man's chamber; there he exhorted his brother, with the piety of a confessor, to repent of his sins and make atonement for them. He made known Sir Philip's proposals, and observed on the wonderful discovery of his crime, and the punishment that followed it. Your repentance, continued he, may be accepted, and your crime may yet be pardoned: If you continue refractory, and refuse to make atonement, you will draw down upon you a severer punishment. The criminal would not confess, and yet could not deny the truth and justice of his observations. The

Baron spent several hours in his brother's chamber; he sent for a priest who took his confession, and they both sat up with him all night, advising, persuading, and exhorting him to do justice, and to comply with the proposals. He was unwilling to give up the world, and yet more so to become the object of public shame, disgrace, and punishment.

The next day Lord Fitz-Owen summoned the company into his brother's chamber, and there declared, in his name, that he accepted Sir Philip Harclay's proposals; that if the young man could, as he promised, direct them to the places where his parents were buried, and if his birth should be authenticated by his foster parents, he should be acknowledged the heir of the house of Lovel. That, to be certified of these things, they must commission proper persons to go with him for this purpose; and, in case the truth should be made plain, they should immediately put him in possession of the castle and estate, in the state it was. He desired Lord Graham and Lord Clifford to choose the commissioners, and gave Sir Philip and Edmund a right to add to them, each, another person.

Lord Graham named the eldest son of Lord Clifford; and the other, in return, named his nephew; they also chose the priest, Lord Graham's confessor, and the eldest son of Baron Fitz-Owen, to his great mortification. Sir Philip appointed Mr. William Fitz-Owen, and Edmund named Father Oswald; they chose out the servants to attend them, who were also to be witnesses of all that should pass. Lord Clifford proposed to Baron Fitz-Owen, that as soon as the commissioners were set out, the remainder of the company should adjourn to his seat in Cumberland, whither Lord Graham should be invited to accompany them, and to stay till this affair was decided. After some debate, this was agreed to; and, at the same time, that the criminal should be kept with them till every thing was properly settled.

Lord Fitz-Owen gave his son William the charge to receive and entertain the commissioners at the castle: But before they set out, Sir Philip had a conference with Lord Fitz-Owen concerning the surrender of the Castle, in which he insisted on the furniture and stock of the farm, in consideration of the arrears. Lord

Fitz-Owen slightly mentioned the young man's education and expences. Sir Philip answered, You are right, my Lord; I had not thought of this point; we owe you in this respect more than we can ever repay: But you know not half the respect and affection Edmund bears for you. When restitution of his title and fortune are fully made, his happiness will still depend on you.—How on me? said the Baron.—Why, he will not be happy unless you honour him with your notice and esteem; but this is not all, I must hope that you will do still more for him.—Indeed, said the Baron; he has put my regard for him to a severe proof, what further can he expect from me?—My dear Lord be not offended, I have only one more proposal to make to you; if you refuse it, I can allow for you; and I confess it requires a greatness of mind, but not more than you possess, to grant it.—Well, Sir, speak your demand?— Say rather my request, It is this: Cease to look upon Edmund as the enemy of your house; look upon him as a son, and make him so indeed!—How say you, Sir Philip? my son!—Yes, my Lord; give him your daughter: He is already your son in filial affection! your son William and he are sworn brothers; what remains but to make him yours? He deserves such a parent, you such a son; and you will, by this means, ingraft* into your family, the name, title and estate of Lovel, which will be entailed on your posterity for ever. This offer requires much consideration, returned the Baron.—Suffer me to suggest some hints to you, said Sir Philip. This match is, I think, verily pointed out by providence, which hath conducted the dear boy through so many dangers, and brought him within view of his happiness; look on him as the precious relick of a noble house, the son of my dearest friend! or look on him as my son and heir, and let me, as his father, implore you to consent to his marriage with your daughter. The Baron's heart was touched, he turned away his face.—Oh Sir Philip Harclay, what a friend are you! why should such a man be our enemy?—My Lord, said Sir Philip, we are not, cannot be enemies: our hearts are already allied; and I am certain we shall one day be dear friends. The Baron suppressed his emotions, but Sir Philip saw into his heart. I must consult my eldest son, returned he.—Then, replied Sir Philip, I foresee much difficulty;

he is prejudiced against Edmund, and thinks the restitution of his inheritance an injury to your family: Hereafter he will see this alliance in a different light, and will rejoice that such a brother is added to the family; but, at present, he will set his face against it. However, we will not despair; virtue and resolution will surmount all obstacles. Let me call in young Lovel.

He brought Edmund to the Baron, and acquainted him with the proposal he had been making in his name, my Lord's answers, and the objections he feared on the part of Sir Robert. Edmund kneeled to the Baron, he took his hand and pressed it to his lips. Best of men! of parents! of patrons! said he, I will ever be your son in filial affection, whether I have the honour to be legally so or not; not one of your own children can feel a stronger sense of love and duty.—Tell me, said the Baron, do you love my daughter?—I do, my Lord, with the most ardent affection; I never loved any woman but her; and if I am so unfortunate as to be refused her, I will not marry at all. Oh, my Lord, reject not my honest suit! Your alliance will give me consequence with myself, it will excite me to act worthy of the station to which I am exalted; if you refuse me, I shall seem an abject wretch, disdained by those whom my heart claims relation to: Your family are the whole world to me. Give me your lovely daughter! give me also your son, my beloved William! and let me share with them the fortune providence bestows upon me: But what is title or fortune, if I am deprived of the society of those I love?

Edmund, said the Baron, you have a noble friend, but you have a stronger in my heart, which I think was implanted there by Heaven to aid its own purposes: I feel a variety of emotions of different kinds, and am afraid to trust my own heart with you. But answer me a question; Are you assured of my daughter's consent? have you solicited her favour? have you gained her affections?—Never, my Lord! I am incapable of so base an action: I have loved her at an humble distance; but, in my situation, I should have thought it a violation of all the laws of gratitude and hospitality, to have presumed to speak the sentiments of my heart.—Then you have acted with unquestionable honour on this, and I must say on all other occasions.—Your approbation, my Lord, is the first wish of my life; it is the seal of my honour and happiness.

Sir Philip smiled: My Lord Fitz-Owen, I am jealous of Edmund's preferable regard for you, it is just the same now as formerly. Edmund came to Sir Philip, he threw himself into his arms, he wept, he was overpowered with the feelings of his heart; he prayed to Heaven to strengthen his mind to support his inexpressible sensations. I am overwhelmed with obligation! said he; Oh, best of friends, teach me, like you, to make my actions speak for me!—Enough Edmund; I know your heart, and that is my security. My Lord, speak to him, and bring him to himself by behaving coldly to him if you can. The Baron said, I must not trust myself with you, you make a child of me! I will only add, Gain my son Robert's favour, and be assured of mine: I owe some respect to the heir of my family, he is brave, honest, and sincere; your enemies are separated from him, you have William's influence in your behalf; make one effort, and let me know the result. Edmund kissed his hand in transports of joy and gratitude.—I will not lose a moment, said he; I fly to obey your commands.

Edmund went immediately to his friend William, and related all that had passed between the Baron, Sir Philip, and himself. William promised him his interest in the warmest manner: He recapitulated all that had passed in the Castle since his departure; but he guarded his sister's delicacy, till it should be resolved to give way to his address. They both consulted young Clifford, who had conceived an affection to Edmund for his amiable qualities, and to William for his generous friendship for him. He promised them his assistance, as Sir Robert seemed desirous to cultivate his friendship. Accordingly, they both attacked him with the whole artillery of friendship and persuasion. Clifford urged the merits of Edmund, and the advantages of his alliance: William enforced his arguments by a retrospect of Edmund's past life; and observed, that every obstacle thrown in his way, had brought his enemies to shame, and increase of honour to himself. I say nothing, continued he, of his noble qualities and affectionate heart; those who have been so many years his companions, can want no proofs of it.—We know your attachment to him Sir, said Sir

Robert: and, in consequence, your partiality.—Nay, replied William, you are sensible of the truth of my assertions; and, I am confident, would have loved him yourself, but for the insinuations of his enemies: But if he should make good his assertions, even you must be convinced of his veracity.—And you would have my father give him your sister upon this uncertainty?—No, Sir, but upon these conditions.—But suppose he does not make them good?—Then I will be of your party, and give up his interest.—Very well, Sir; my father may do as he pleases; but I cannot agree to give my sister to one who has always stood in the way of our family, and now turns us out of our own house.

I am sorry, brother, you see his pretensions in so wrong a light; but if you think there is any imposture in the case, go with us, and be a witness of all that passes?—No, not I! if Edmund is to be master of the Castle, I will never more set my foot in it.—This matter, said Mr. Clifford, must be left to time, which has brought stranger things to pass. Sir Robert's honour and good sense will enable him to subdue his prejudices, and to judge impartially. They took leave, and went to make preparations for their journey.

Edmund made his report of Sir Robert's inflexibility to his father, in presence of Sir Philip; who, again, ventured to urge the Baron on his favourite subject. It becomes me to wait for the further proofs, said he; but if they are as clear as I expect, I will not be inexorable to your wishes: Say nothing more on this subject till the return of the commissioners. They were profuse in their acknowledgments of his goodness.

Edmund took a tender leave of his two paternal friends: When, said he, I take possession of my inheritance, I must hope for the company of you both to compleat my happiness.—Of me, said Sir Philip, you may be certain; and, as far as my influence reaches, of the Baron.—He was silent. Edmund assured them of his constant prayers for their happiness.

Soon after, the commissioners, with Edmund, set out for Lovel Castle; and the following day the Lord Clifford set out for his own house, with Baron Fitz-Owen and his son. The nominal Baron* was carried with them, very much against his will. Sir Philip Harclay was invited to go with them by Lord Clifford, who declared his presence necessary to bring things to a conclusion. They all joined in acknowledging their obligations to Lord Graham's generous hospitality, and besought him to accompany them; at length he consented, on condition they would allow him to go to and fro, as his duty should call him.

Lord Clifford received them with the greatest hospitality, and presented them to his Lady and three daughters, who were in the bloom of youth and beauty. They spent their time very pleasantly, excepting the criminal, who continued gloomy and reserved, and declined company.

In the mean time the commissioners proceeded on their journey. When they were within a day's distance from the Castle, Mr. William and his servant put forward, and arrived several hours before the rest, to make preparations for their reception. His sister and brother received them with open arms, and enquired eagerly after the event of the journey to the north. He gave them a brief account of every thing that had happened to their uncle; adding, but this is not all: Sir Philip Harclay has brought a young man, whom he pretends is the son of the late Lord Lovel, and claims his estate and title. This person is on his journey hither, with several others who are commissioned to enquire into certain particulars, to confirm his pretensions:—If he make good his claim, my father will surrender the Castle and estate into his hands. Sir Philip and my Lord have many points to settle; and he has proposed a compromise that you, my sister, ought to know, because it nearly concerns you.—Me! brother William; pray explain yourself!—Why, he proposes that in lieu of arrears and other expectations, my father shall give his dear Emma to the heir of Lovel, in full of all demands.—She changed colour: Holy Mary! said she; and does my father agree to this proposal?—He is not very averse to it; but Sir Robert refuses his consent: However, I have given him my interest with you.—Have you indeed? What! a stranger, perhaps an impostor, who comes to turn us out of our dwelling?—Have patience, my Emma! see this young man without prejudice, and perhaps you will like him as well as I do.—I am surprised at you, William!—Dear Emma, I cannot bear to see you uneasy. Think of the man who of all others you would wish to see in a situation to ask you of your father, and expect to see your wishes realized.—Impossible! said she.—Nothing is impossible, my dear; let us be prudent, and all will end happily. You must help me to receive and entertain these commissioners. I expect a very solemn scene; but when that is once got over, happier hours than the past will succeed. We shall first visit the haunted apartment; you, my sister, will keep in your own till I shall send for you. I go now to give orders to the servants. He went and ordered them to be in waiting; and himself, and his youngest brother, stood in readiness to receive them.

The sound of the horn announced the arrival of the commissioners; at the same instant a sudden gust of wind arose, and the outward gates flew open. They entered the court-yard, and the great folding doors into the hall, were opened without any assistance. The moment Edmund entered the hall, every door in the house flew open; the servants all rushed into the hall, and fear was written on their countenances: Joseph only was undaunted. These doors, said he, open of their own accord to receive their master! this is he indeed!—Edmund was soon apprized of what had happened.—I accept the omen! said he. Gentlemen, let us go forward to the apartment! let us finish the work of fate! I will lead the way. He went on to the apartment, followed by all present. Open the shutters, said he, the day-light shall no longer be excluded here; the deeds of darkness shall now be brought to light.

They descended the staircase; every door was open, till they came to the fatal closet. Edmund called to Mr. William: Approach, my friend, and behold the door your family overlooked! They came forward; he drew the key out of his bosom and unlocked the door; he made them observe that the boards were all loose; he then called to the servants, and bid them remove every thing out of the closet. While they were doing this, Edmund shewed them the breast-plate all stained with blood; he then called to Joseph: Do you know whose was this suit of armour?—It was my Lord's, said Joseph; the late Lord Lovel; I have seen him wear it.

Edmund bade them bring shovels and remove the earth. While

they were gone, he desired Oswald to repeat all that passed the night they sat up together in that apartment, which he did till the servants returned. They threw out the earth, while the bye-standers in solemn silence waited the event. After some time and labour they struck against something. They proceeded till they discovered a large trunk, which with some difficulty they drew out. It had been corded round, but the cords were rotted to dust. They opened it, and found a skeleton which appeared to have been tied neck and heels together, and forced into the trunk. Behold, said Edmund, the bones of him to whom I owe my birth! The priest from Lord Graham's advanced.—This is undoubtedly the body of the Lord Lovel; I heard his kinsman confess the manner in which he was interred. Let this awful spectacle be a lesson to all present, that though wickedness may triumph for a season, a day of retribution will come! Oswald exclaimed—Behold the day of retribution! of triumph to the innocent, of shame and confusion to the wicked.

The young gentlemen declared that Edmund had made good his assertions; what then, said they, remains? I propose, said Lord Graham's priest, that an account be written of this discovery, and signed by all the witnesses present; that an attested copy be left in the hands of this gentleman, and the original be sent to the Barons and Sir Philip Harclay, to convince them of the truth of it.

Mr. Clifford then desired Edmund to proceed in his own way. The first thing I propose to do, said he, is to have a coffin made for these honoured remains; I trust to find the bones of my other parent, and to inter them all together in consecrated ground. Unfortunate pair! you shall at last rest together! your son shall pay the last duties to your ashes! He stopped to shed tears, and none present but paid this tribute to their misfortunes. Edmund recovered his voice and proceeded—My next request is, that Father Oswald and this reverend father, with whoever else the gentlemen shall appoint, will send for Andrew and Margery Twyford, and examine them concerning the circumstances of my birth, and the death and burial of my unfortunate mother.—It shall be done, said Mr. William; but first let me intreat you to come with me and take some refreshment after your journey, for you must be fatigued: After dinner we will proceed in the enquiry.

They all followed him into the great hall, where they were entertained with great hospitality, and Mr. William did the honours in his father's name. Edmund's heart was deeply affected, and the solemnity of his deportment bore witness to his sincerity; but it was a manly sorrow, that did not make him neglect his duty to his friends or himself. He enquired after the health of the lady Emma. She is well, said William, and as much your friend as ever. Edmund bowed in silence.

After dinner the commissioners sent for Andrew and his wife. They examined them separately, and found their accounts agreed together, and were in substance the same as Oswald and Edmund had before related, separately also. The commissioners observed, that there could be no collusion between them, and that the proofs were indisputable. They kept the foster parents all night; and the next day Andrew directed them to the place where the Lady Lovel was buried, between two trees which he had marked for a memorial. They collected the bones and carried them to the Castle, where Edmund caused a stately coffin to be made for the remains of the unfortunate pair. The two priests obtained leave to look in the coffin buried in the church, and found nothing but stones and earth in it. The commissioners then declared they were fully satisfied of the reality of Edmund's pretensions.

The two priests were employed in drawing up a circumstantial account of these discoveries, in order to make their report to the Barons at their return. In the mean time Mr. William took an opportunity to introduce Edmund to his sister. My Emma, said he, the heir of Lovel is desirous to pay his respects to you. They were both in apparent confusion; but Edmund's wore off, and Emma's increased. I have been long desirous, said he, to pay my respects to the Lady whom I most honour, but unavoidable duties have detained me; when these are fully paid, it is my wish to devote the remainder of my life to Lady Emma!—Are you, then, the heir of Lovel?—I am, Madam; and am also the man in whose behalf I once presumed to speak.—'Tis very strange indeed!—It is so, Madam, to myself; but time that reconciles us to all things,

will, I hope, render this change in my situation familiar to you.
William said, you are both well acquainted with the wishes of
my heart; but my advice is, that you do not encourage a farther
intimacy till my Lord's determination be fully known.—You may
dispose of me as you please, said Edmund; but I cannot help
declaring my wishes; yet I will submit to my Lord's sentence
though he should doom me to despair.

From this period, the young pair behaved with solemn respect
to each other, but with apparent reserve. The young Lady sometimes appeared in company, but oftener chose to be in her own
apartment, where she began to believe and hope for the comple-
tion of her wishes. The uncertainty of the Baron's determination,
threw an air of anxiety over Edmund's face: His friend William,
by the most tender care and attentions, strove to dispel his fears,
and encourage his hopes; but he waited with impatience for the
return of the commissioners, and the decision of his fate.

While these things passed at the Castle of Lovel, the nominal
Baron recovered his health and strength at the house of Lord
Clifford: In the same proportion he grew more and more shy and
reserved, avoided the company of his brother and nephew, and
was frequently shut up with his two servants. Sir Robert Fitz-
Owen made several attempts to gain his confidence, but in vain;
he was equally shy to him as the rest. M. Zadisky observed his
motions with the penetration for which his countrymen have
been distinguished in all ages: He communicated his suspicions
to Sir Philip and the Barons, giving it as his opinion, that the
criminal was meditating an escape. They asked, what he thought
was to be done? Zadisky offered to watch him in turn with
another person, and to lye in wait for him; he also proposed, that
horses should be kept in readiness, and men to mount them,
without knowledge of the service they were to be employed in.
The Barons agreed to leave the whole management of this affair
to Zadisky. He took his measures so well, that he intercepted the
three fugitives in the fields adjoining to the house, and brought
them all back prisoners. They confined them separately, while the
Lords and Gentlemen consulted how to dispose of them.

Sir Philip applied to Lord Fitz-Owen, who begged leave to be silent: I have nothing, said he, to offer in favour of this bad man; and I cannot propose harsher measures with so near a relation. Zadisky then begged to be heard, You can no longer have any reliance upon the word of a man who has forfeited all pretensions to honour and sincerity. I have long wished to revisit once more my native country, and to enquire after some very dear friends I left there; I will undertake to convey this man to a very distant part of the world, where it will be out of his power to do further mischief, and free his relations from an ungrateful charge, unless you should rather chuse to bring him to punishment here. Lord Clifford approved of the proposal; Lord Fitz-Owen remained silent, but shewed no marks of disapprobation.

Sir Philip objected to parting with his friend; but Zadisky assured him he had particular reasons for returning to the Holy Land, of which he should be judge hereafter. Sir Philip desired the Lord Fitz-Owen to give him his company to the criminal's apartment, saying, we will have one more conversation with him, and that shall decide his fate. They found him silent and sullen, and he refused to answer their questions.—Sir Philip then bespoke him.—After the proofs you have given of your falsehood and insincerity, we can no longer have any reliance upon you, nor faith in your fulfilling the conditions of our agreement; I will, therefore, once more make you a proposal that shall still leave you indebted to our clemency. You shall banish yourself from England for ever, and go in pilgrimage to the Holy Land, with such companions as we shall appoint; or, secondly, you shall enter directly into a monastery, and there be shut up for life; or, thirdly, if you refuse both these offers, I will go directly to Court, throw myself at the feet of my Sovereign, relate the whole story of your wicked life and actions, and demand vengeance on your head. The King is too good and pious to let such villany go unpunished; he will bring you to public shame and punishment: And be you assured, if I begin this prosecution, I will pursue it to the utmost. I appeal to your worthy brother for the justice of my proceeding. I reason no more with you, I only declare my resolution. I wait your answer one hour, and the next I put in execution whatever you shall oblige me to determine. So saying they retired, and left him to reflect and to resolve. At the expiration of the hour they sent Zadisky to receive his answer; he insinuated to him the generosity and charity of Sir Philip and the Lords, and the certainty of their resolutions, and begged him to take care what answer he returned, for that his fate depended on it. He kept silent several minutes, resentment and despair were painted on his visage; at length he spoke:

Tell my proud enemies that I prefer banishment to death, infamy, or a life of solitude.—You have chosen well, said Zadisky. To a wise man all countries are alike; it shall be my care to make mine agreeable to you.—Are you, then, the person chosen for my companion?—I am, Sir; and you may judge by that circumstance, that those whom you call your enemies, are not so in effect. Farewell, Sir; I go to prepare for our departure.

Zadisky went and made his report, and then set immediately about his preparations. He chose two active young men for his attendants; and gave them directions to keep a strict eye upon their charge, for that they should be accountable if he should escape them.

In the mean time the Baron Fitz-Owen had several conferences with his brother; he endeavoured to make him sensible of his crimes, and of the justice and clemency of his Conqueror; but he was moody and reserved to him as to the rest. Sir Philip Harclay obliged him to surrender his worldly estates into the hands of Lord Fitz-Owen: A writing was drawn up for that purpose, and executed in the presence of them all. Lord Fitz-Owen engaged to allow him an annual sum, and to advance money for the expences of his voyage. He spoke to him in the most affectionate manner, but he refused his embrace: You will have nothing to regret, said he, haughtily; for the gain is yours. Sir Philip conjured Zadisky to return to him again; who answered, I will either return, or give such reasons for my stay, as you shall approve. I will send a messenger to acquaint you with my arrival in Syria, and with such other particulars as I shall judge interesting to you and yours. In the mean time remember me in your prayers, and preserve for me those sentiments of friendship and esteem, that I have always deemed one of the chief honours and blessings of my life.—Commend my love and duty to your adopted son; he will more than supply my absence, and be the comfort of your old age. Adieu, best and noblest of friends!—They took a tender leave of each other, not without tears on both sides.

The travellers set out directly for a distant seaport, where they heard of a ship bound for the Levant, in which they embarked and proceeded on their voyage.

The Commissioners arrived at Lord Clifford's a few days after the departure of the adventurers. They gave a minute account of their commission, and expressed themselves entirely satisfied of the justice of Edmund's pretensions; they gave an account in writing of all that they had been eye-witness to, and ventured to urge the Baron Fitz-Owen on the subject of Edmund's wishes. The Baron was already disposed in his favour; his mind was employed in the future establishment of his family. During their residence at Lord Clifford's, his eldest son Sir Robert had cast his eye upon the eldest daughter of that nobleman, and he besought his father to ask her in marriage for him. The Baron was pleased with the alliance, and took the first opportunity to mention it to Lord Clifford; who answered him, pleasantly, I will give my daughter to your son, upon condition that you will give yours to the Heir of Lovel. The Baron looked serious: Lord Clifford went on—I like that young man so well, that I would accept him for a son-in-law, if he asked me for my daughter; and if I have any influence with you I will use it in his behalf.—A powerful solicitor indeed! said the Baron; but you know my eldest son's reluctance to it; if he consents, so will I.—He shall consent, said Lord Clifford, or he shall have no daughter of mine. Let him subdue his prejudices, and then I will lay aside my scruples.— But, my Lord, replied the Baron, if I can obtain his free consent, it will be the best for all: I will try once more, and if he will not, I will leave it wholly to your management.

When the noble company were all assembled, Sir Philip Harclay revived the subject, and besought the Lord Fitz-Owen to put an end to the work he had begun, by confirming Edmund's happiness. The Baron rose up, and thus spoke: The proofs of Edmund's noble birth, the still stronger ones of his excellent endowments and qualities, the solicitations of so many noble friends in his behalf, have altogether determined me in his favour; and I hope to do justice to his merit, without detriment to my other children: I am resolved to make them all as happy as my power will allow me to do. Lord Clifford has been so gracious to promise his fair daughter to my son Robert, upon certain conditions, that I will take upon me to ratify, and which will render my son worthy of the happiness that awaits him. My children are the undoubted heirs of my unhappy brother, Lovel; you, my son, shall therefore immediately take possession of your Uncle's house and estate, only obliging you to pay to each of your younger brothers, the sum of one thousand pounds; on this condition I will secure that estate to you and your heirs for ever. I will by my own act and deed surrender the Castle and estate of Lovel to the right owner, and at the same time marry him to my daughter. I will settle a proper allowance upon my two younger sons, and dispose of what remains by a will and testament; and then I shall have done all my business in this world, and shall have nothing to do but prepare for the next.

Oh my father! said Sir Robert, I cannot bear your generosity! you would give away all to others, and reserve nothing for yourself.—Not so, my son, said the Baron: I will repair my old castle in Wales, and reside there. I will visit my children, and be visited by them; I will enjoy their happiness, and by that means increase my own; whether I look backwards or forwards I shall have nothing to do but rejoice, and be thankful to Heaven that has given me so many blessings: I shall have the comfortable reflection of having discharged my duties as a citizen, a husband, a father, a friend; and, whenever I am summoned away from this world, I shall die content.

Sir Robert came forward with tears on his cheeks, he kneeled to his father—Best of parents, and of men! said he, you have subdued a heart that has been too refractory to your will; you have this day made me sensible how much I owe to your goodness and forbearance with me. Forgive me all that is past, and from henceforward dispose of me; I will have no will but yours, no ambition but to be worthy of the name of your son.—And this day, said the Baron, do I enjoy the true happiness of a father! Rise, my son, and take possession of the first place in my affection without reserve. They embraced with tears on both sides: The company rose, and congratulated both father and son. The Baron presented his son to Lord Clifford, who embraced him, and said, You shall have my daughter, for I see that you deserve her.

Sir Philip Harclay approached; the Baron gave his son's hand to the knight:—Love and respect that good man, said he; deserve his friendship, and you will obtain it. Nothing but congratulations were heard on all sides.

When their joy was in some degree reduced to composure, Sir Philip proposed that they should begin to execute the schemes of happiness they had planned. He proposed that my Lord Fitz-Owen should go with him to the Castle of Lovel, and settle the family there. The Baron consented; and both together invited such of the company as liked it, to accompany them thither. It was agreed that a nephew of Lord Graham's, another of Lord Clifford's, two Gentlemen, friends of Sir Philip Harclay, and Father Oswald, should be of the party; together with several of Sir Philip's dependants and domestics, and the attendants on the rest. Lord Fitz-Owen gave orders for their speedy departure. Lord Graham and his friends took leave of them, in order to return to his own home; but before he went, he engaged his eldest nephew and heir to the second daughter of the Lord Clifford: Sir Robert offered himself to the eldest, who modestly received his address, and made no objection to his proposal. The fathers confirmed their engagement.

Lord Fitz-Owen promised to return to the celebration of the marriage; in the mean time he ordered his son to go and take possession of his Uncle's house, and to settle his household: He invited young Clifford, and some other Gentlemen, to go with him. The company separated with regret, and with many promises of friendship on all sides; and the Gentlemen of the North were to cultivate the good neighbourhood on both sides of the borders.

Sir Philip Harclay and the Baron Fitz-Owen, with their friends and attendants, set forwards for the Castle of Lovel; a servant went before, at full speed, to acquaint the family of their approach. Edmund was in great anxiety of mind, now the crisis of his fate was near at hand: He enquired of the messenger, who were of the party? and finding that Sir Philip Harclay was there, and that Sir Robert Fitz-Owen staid in the North, his hopes rose above his fears. Mr. William, attended by a servant, rode forward to meet them; he desired Edmund to stay and receive them. Edmund was under some difficulty with regard to his behaviour to the lovely Emma; a thousand times his heart rose to his lips, as often he suppressed his emotions; they both sighed frequently, said little, thought much, and wished for the event. Master Walter was too young to partake of their anxieties, but he wished for the arrival of his father to end them.

Mr. William's impatience spurred him on to meet his father; as soon as he saw him, he rode up directly to him: My dear father, you are welcome home! said he.—I think not, Sir, said the Baron, and looked serious.—Why so, my Lord? said William.—Because it is no longer mine, but another man's home, answered he, and I must receive my welcome from him. Meaning Edmund? said William.—Whom else can it be?—Ah, my Lord! he is your creature, your servant, he puts his fate into your hands, and will submit to your pleasure in all things!—Why comes he not to meet us? said the Baron.—His fears prevent him, said William; but speak the word, and I will fetch him?—No, said the Baron, we will wait on him.—William looked confused: Is Edmund so unfortunate, said he, as to have incurred your displeasure? Sir Philip Harclay advanced, and laid his hand on William's saddle—Generous impatience! noble youth! said he; look round you, and see if you can discover in this company one enemy of your friend? Leave to your excellent father the time and manner of explaining himself; he only can do justice to his own sentiments. The Baron smiled on Sir Philip: William's countenance cleared up; they went forward, and soon arrived at the Castle of Lovel.

Edmund was walking to and fro in the hall, when he heard the horn that announced their arrival; his emotions were so great that he could hardly support them. The Baron and Sir Philip entered the hall hand in hand; Edmund threw himself at their feet and embraced their knees, but could not utter a word. They raised him between them, and strove to encourage him; but he threw himself into the arms of Sir Philip Harclay, deprived of strength, and almost of life. They supported him to a seat, where he recovered by degrees, but had no power to speak his feelings; he looked up to his Benefactors in the most affecting manner, he laid his hand upon his bosom, but was still silent. Compose yourself, my dear son, said Sir Philip; you are in the arms of your best friends. Look up to the happiness that awaits you, enjoy the blessings that Heaven sends you; lift up your heart in gratitude to the Creator, and think less of what you owe to the creature! You will have time enough to pay us your acknowledgments hereafter.

The company came round them, the servants flocked into the hall, shouts of joy were heard on all sides; the Baron came and took Edmund's hand: Rise, Sir, said he, and do the honours of your house! it is yours from this day: We are your guests, and expect from you our welcome! Edmund kneeled to the Baron, he spoke with a faltering voice—My Lord, I am yours! all that I have is at your devotion! dispose of me as it pleases you best. The Baron embraced him with the greatest affection: Look round you, said he, and salute your friends; these Gentlemen came hither to do you honour. Edmund revived, he embraced and welcomed the Gentlemen. Father Oswald received his embrace with peculiar affection, and gave him his benediction in a most affecting manner: Edmund exclaimed—Pray for me, Father! that I may bear all these blessings with gratitude and moderation! He then saluted and shook hands with all the servants, not omitting the meanest; he distinguished Joseph by a cordial embrace, he called him his dear friend: Now, said he, I can return your friendship, and I am proud to acknowledge it! The old man, with a faltering voice, cried out—Now I have lived long enough! I have seen my master's son acknowledged for the heir of Lovel! the hall echoed with his words: Long live the heir of Lovel!

The Baron took Edmund's hands in his own: Let us retire from this croud, said he; we have business of a more private nature to transact. He led to the parlour, followed by Sir Philip and the other Gentlemen.—Where are my other children? said he. William retired, and presently returned with his brother and sister. They kneeled to their father, who raised and embraced them.—He then called out, William!—Edmund!—come and receive my blessing also: They approached hand in hand, they kneeled, and he gave them a solemn benediction—Your friendship deserves our praise, my children! love each other always! and may Heaven pour down its choicest blessings upon your heads! They rose, and embraced in silent raptures of joy. Edmund presented his friend to Sir Philip: I understand you, said he; this Gentleman was my first acquaintance of this family, he has a title to the second place in my heart: I shall tell him, at more leisure, how much I love and honour him for his own sake as well as yours. He embraced the youth, and desired his friendship.

Come hither, my Emma! said the Baron. She approached, with tears on her cheek, sweetly blushing, like the damask rose, wet with the dew of the morning. I must ask you a serious question, my child; answer me with the same sincerity you would to Heaven. You see this young man, the Heir of Lovel! you have known him long; consult your own heart, and tell me whether you have any objection to receive him for your husband? I have promised to all this company to give you to him; but upon condition that you approve him: I think him worthy of you; and, whether you accept him or not, he shall ever be to me a son; but Heaven forbid that I should compel my child to give her hand where she cannot bestow her heart! Speak freely, and decide this point for me and for yourself. The fair Emma blushed, and was under some confusion; her virgin modesty prevented her speaking for some moments. Edmund trembled, he leaned upon William's shoulder to support himself. Emma cast her eye upon him, she saw his emotion, and hastened to relieve him; she thus spoke, in a soft voice which gathered strength as she proceeded— My Lord and father's goodness has always prevented my wishes; I am the happiest of all children, in being able to obey his commands, without offering violence to my own inclinations: As I am called upon in this public manner, it is but justice to this Gentleman's merit to declare, that, were I at liberty to choose a husband from all the world, he only should be my choice, who I can say, with joy, is my father's also. Edmund bowed low, he advanced towards her; the Baron took his daughter's hand, and presented it to him; he kneeled upon one knee, he took her hand, kissed it, and pressed it to his bosom: The Baron embraced and blessed them; he presented them to Sir Philip Harclay—Receive and acknowledge your children! said he.—I do receive them as the gift of Heaven! said the noble Knight; they are as much mine as if I had begotten them: All that I have is theirs, and shall descend to their children for ever. A fresh scene of congratulation ensued; and the hearts of all the auditors were too much engaged to be able soon to return to the ease and tranquillity of common life.

After they had refreshed themselves, and recovered from the emotions they had sustained on this interesting occasion, Edmund thus addressed the Baron:—On the brink of happiness I must claim your attention to a melancholy subject. The bones of both my parents lie unburied in this house; permit me, my honoured Lord, to perform my last duties to them, and the remainder of my life shall be devoted to you and yours.— Certainly, said the Baron; why have you not interred them?—My Lord, I waited for your arrival, that you might be certified of the reality, and that no doubts might remain.—I have no doubts, said the Baron: Alas, both the crime and punishment of the offender leave no room for them!—He sighed.—Let us now put an end to this affair; and, if possible, forget it for ever.

If it will not be too painful to you my Lord, I would intreat you, with these Gentlemen our friends, to follow me into the east apartment, the scene of my parents' woes, and yet the dawning of my better hopes.

They rose to attend him; he committed the Lady Emma to the care of her youngest brother, observing that the scene was too solemn for a Lady to be present at it. They proceeded to the apartment; he shewed the Baron the fatal closet, and the place where the bones were found, also the trunk that contained them; he recapitulated all that passed before their arrival; he shewed them the coffin where the bones of the unfortunate pair were deposited: He then desired the Baron to give orders for their interment. No, replied he, it belongs to you to order, and every one here is ready to perform it. Edmund then desired Father Oswald to give notice to the Friars of the Monastery of St. Austin, that, with their permission, the funeral should be solemnized there, and the bones interred in the church. He also gave orders that the closet should be floored, the apartment repaired, and put in order. He then returned to the other side of the Castle.

Preparations being made for the funeral, it was performed a few days after. Edmund attended in person as chief-mourner, Sir Philip Harclay as the second; Joseph desired he might assist, as servant to the deceased: They were followed by most people of the village. The story was now become public, and every one blessed Edmund for the piety and devotion with which he performed the last duties to his parents.—Edmund appeared in deep mourning; the week after he assisted at a mass for the repose of the deceased.

Sir Philip Harclay ordered a monument to be erected to the memory of his friends, with the following inscription.

'Praye for the soules of Arthur Lord Lovele and Marie his wife, who were cut off in the flowere of theire youthe, by the trecherye and crueltie of theire neare kinnesmanne. Edmunde theire onlie sonne, one and twentie yeares after theire deathe, by the direction of Heavene, made the discoverye of the mannere of theire deathe, and at the same time proved his owne birthe. He collected theire bones together, and interred them in this place:— A warning and proofe to late posteritie, of the justice of Providence, and the certaintie of Retribution.'*

The Sunday after the funeral, Edmund threw off his mourning, and appeared in a dress suitable to his condition. He received the compliments of his friends with ease and chearfulness, and began to enjoy his happiness. He asked an audience of his fair Mistress, and was permitted to declare the passion he had so long stifled in his own bosom. She gave him a favourable hearing, and in a short time confessed that she had suffered equally in that suspense that was so grievous to him. They engaged themselves by mutual vows to each other, and only waited the Baron's pleasure to complete their happiness; every cloud was vanished from their brows, and sweet tranquillity took possession of their bosoms. Their friends shared their happiness; William and Edmund renewed their vows of everlasting friendship, and promised to be as much together as William's other duties would permit.

The Baron once more summoned all his company together; he told Edmund all that had passed relating to his brother-in-law, his exile, and the pilgrimage of Zadisky; he then related the circumstances of Sir Robert's engagement to Lord Clifford's daughter, his establishment in his Uncle's seat, and his own obligations to return time enough to be present at the marriage: But before I go, said he, I will give my daughter to the Heir of Lovel, and then I shall have discharged my duty to him, and my promise to Sir Philip Harclay.

You have nobly performed both, said Sir Philip, and whenever you depart I shall be your companion.—What, said Edmund, am I to be deprived of both my fathers at once? My honoured Lord, you have given away two houses, where do you intend to reside?—No matter, said the Baron; I know I shall be welcome to both.—My dear Lord, said Edmund, stay here and be still the Master; I shall be proud to be under your command, and to be your servant as well as your son!—No Edmund, said the Baron, that would not now be proper; this is your Castle, you are its Lord and Master, and it is incumbent on you to shew yourself worthy of the great things Providence has done for you.—How shall I, a young man, acquit myself of so many duties as will be upon me, without the advice and assistance of my two paternal friends? Oh, Sir Philip! will you too leave me? once you gave me hopes—he stopped, greatly affected. Sir Philip said, Tell me truly, Edmund, do you really desire that I should live with you?—As truly, Sir, as I desire life and happiness!—Then, my dear child, I will live and die with you! They embraced with tears of affection, and Edmund was all joy and gratitude. My good Lord, said Sir Philip, you have disposed of two houses, and have none ready to receive you; will you accept of mine? it is much at your service, and its being in the same county with your eldest son, will be an inducement to you to reside there. The Baron caught Sir Philip's hand—Noble Sir, I thank you, and I will embrace your kind offer;

I will be your tenant for the present; my castle in Wales shall be put in repair, in the mean time; if I do not reside there, it will be an establishment for one of my younger sons: But what will you do with your old soldiers and dependants?—My Lord, I will never cast them off. There is another house on my estate that has been shut up many years; I will have it repaired and furnished properly for the reception of my old men: I will endow it with a certain sum to be paid annually, and will appoint a steward to manage their revenue; I will continue it during the lives of the first inhabitants, and after that I shall leave it to my son here, to do as he pleases.—Your son, said Edmund, will make it the business of his life to act worthy of such a father.—Enough, said Sir Philip, I am satisfied that you will. I purpose to reside myself in that very apartment which my dear friend your father inhabited; I will tread in his footsteps, and think he sees me acting his part in his son's family. I will be attended by my own servants; and, whenever you desire it, I will give you my company; your joys, your griefs shall be mine, I shall hold your children in my arms, and their prattle shall amuse my old age: And, as my last earthly wish, your hands shall close my eyes.—Long, very long, said Edmund (with eyes and hands lifted up), may it be ere I perform so sad a duty!—Long and happily may you live together, said the Baron! I will hope to see you sometimes, and to claim a share in your blessings. But let us give no more tears to sorrow, the rest shall be those of joy and transport. The first step we take shall be to marry our Edmund; I will give orders for the celebration, and they shall be the last orders I shall give in this house. They then separated, and went to prepare for the approaching solemnity.

Sir Philip and the Baron had a private conference concerning Edmund's assuming the name and title of Lovel. I am resolved, said Sir Philip, to go to the King; to acquaint him briefly with Edmund's history; I will request that he may be called up to parliament by a writ, for there is no need of a new patent, he being the true inheritor; in the mean time he shall assume the name, arms, and title, and I will answer any one that shall dispute his right to them. Sir Philip then declared his resolution to set out with the Baron at his departure, and to settle all his other affairs before he returned to take up his residence at the Castle.

A few days after, the marriage was celebrated to the entire satisfaction of all parties. The Baron ordered the doors to be thrown open, and the house free for all comers; with every other token of joy and festivity. Edmund appeared full of joy without levity, of mirth without extravagance; he received the congratulations of his friends, with ease, freedom and vivacity. He sent for his foster father and mother, who began to think themselves neglected, as he had been so deeply engaged in affairs of more consequence that he had not been particularly attentive to them; he made them come into the great hall, and presented them to his Lady.

These, said he, are the good people to whom I am, under God, indebted for my present happiness; they were my first benefactors; I was obliged to them for food and sustenance in my childhood, and this good woman nourished my infancy at her own breast. The Lady received them graciously, and saluted Margery. Andrew kneeled down, and with great humility, begged Edmund's pardon for his treatment of him in his childhood. I heartily forgive you, said he, and I will excuse you to yourself; it was natural for you to look upon me as an intruder, that was eating your children's bread; you saved my life, and afterwards you sustained it by your food and raiment: I ought to have maintained myself, and to have contributed to your maintenance. But, besides this, your treatment of me was the first of my preferment; it recommended me to the notice of this noble family: Every thing that happened to me since, has been a step to my present state of honour and happiness. Never man had so many benefactors as myself; but both they, and myself, have been only instruments in the hands of providence, to bring about its own purposes: Let us praise God for all! I shared your poverty, and you will share my riches; I will give you the cottage where you dwell, and the ground about it; I will also pay you the annual sum of ten pounds for the lives of you both; I will put out your children to manual trades, and assist you to provide for them in their own station; and you are to look upon this as paying a debt, and not bestowing a gift: I owe you more than I can ever pay; and, if there be any thing further in my power that will contribute to your happiness, you can ask nothing in reason that I will deny you.

Andrew hid his face: I cannot bear it! said he; Oh what a brute was I, to abuse such a child as this! I shall never forgive myself!—You must indeed, my friend, for I forgive and thank you. Andrew retired back, but Margery came forward; she looked earnestly on Edmund, she then threw her arms about his neck, and wept aloud—My precious child! my lovely babe! thank God, I have lived to see this day! I will rejoice in your good fortune, and your bounty to us, but I must ask one more favour yet; that I may sometimes come hither and behold that gracious countenance, and thank God that I was honoured so far as to give thee food from my own breast, and to bring thee up to be a blessing to me, and to all that know thee! Edmund was affected, he returned her embrace; he bade her come to the Castle as often as she pleased, and she should always be received as his mother; the bride saluted her, and told her the oftener she came, the more welcome she should be. Margery and her husband retired, full of blessings and prayers for their happiness; she gave vent to her joy, by relating to the servants and neighbours every circumstance of Edmund's birth, infancy, and childhood: Many a tear was dropped by the auditors, and many a prayer wafted to Heaven for his happiness. Joseph took up the story where she left it; he told the rising dawn of youth and virtue, darting its ray through the clouds of obscurity, and how every stroke of envy and malignity brushed away some part of the darkness that veiled its lustre: He told the story of the haunted apartment, and all the consequences of it; how he and Oswald conveyed the youth away from the castle, no more to return till he came as master of it: He closed the tale with praise to Heaven for the happy discovery, that gave such an heir to the house of Lovel; to his dependants such a Lord and Master; to mankind a friend and benefactor. There was truly a house of joy; not that false kind, in the midst of which there is heaviness, but that of rational creatures grateful to the supreme benefactor, raising their minds by a due enjoyment of earthly blessings to a preparation for a more perfect state hereafter.

A few days after the wedding, the Lord Fitz-Owen began to prepare for his journey to the north. He gave to Edmund the plate, linen, and furniture of the Castle, the farming stock and utensils; he would have added a sum of money, but Sir Philip stopped his hand: We do not forget, said he, that you have other children, we will not suffer you to injure them; give us your blessing and paternal affection, and we have nothing more to ask: I told you, my Lord, that you and I should one day be sincere friends.—We must be so, answered the Baron; it is impossible to be long your enemy: We are brothers, and shall be to our lives end.

They regulated the young man's household; the Baron gave leave to the servants to choose their master; the elder ones followed him (except Joseph, who desired to live with Edmund, as the chief happiness of his life); most of the younger ones chose the service of the youthful pair. There was a tender and affectionate parting on all sides. Edmund besought his beloved William not to leave him. The Baron said, he must insist on his being at his brother's wedding, as a due attention to him; but after that he should return to the Castle for some time.

The Baron and Sir Philip Harclay, with their train, set forward. Sir Philip went to London and obtained all he desired for his Edmund; from thence he went into Yorkshire, and settled his affairs there, removing his pensioners to his other house, and putting Lord Fitz-Owen in possession of his own. They had a generous contention about the terms; but Sir Philip insisted on the Baron's accepting the use of every thing there: You hold it in trust for a future grandchild, said he, whom I hope to live to endow with it.

During Sir Philip's absence, the young Lord Lovel caused the haunted apartment to be repaired and furnished for the reception of his father by adoption. He placed his friend Joseph over all his men servants, and ordered him to forbear his attendance; but the old man would always stand at the side-board, and feast his eyes with the countenance of his own Master's son, surrounded with honour and happiness. John Wyatt waited upon the person of his Lord, and enjoyed his favour without abatement. Mr. William Fitz-Owen accompanied Sir Philip Harclay from the north country, when he returned to take up his residence at the Castle of Lovel.

Edmund, in the arms of love and friendship, enjoyed with true relish the blessings that surrounded him, with an heart overflowing with benevolence to his fellow-creatures, and raptures of gratitude to his Creator. His Lady and himself were examples of conjugal affection and happiness. Within a year from his marriage she brought him a son and heir, whose birth renewed the joy and congratulations of all his friends: The Baron Fitz-Owen came to the baptism, and partook of his children's blessings. The child was called Arthur, after the name of his grandfather.

The year following was born a second son, who was called Philip Harclay; upon him the noble knight of that name settled his estate in Yorkshire; and by the king's permission, he took the name and arms of that family.

The third son was called William; he inherited the fortune of his uncle of that name, who adopted him, and he made the Castle of Lovel his residence, and died a batchelor.

The fourth son was called Edmund; the fifth Owen; and there was also a daughter called Emma.

When time had worn out the prejudices of Sir Robert Fitz-Owen, the good old Baron of that name proposed a marriage between his eldest son and heir, and the daughter of Edmund Lord Lovel, which was happily concluded. The nuptials were honoured with the presence of both families; and the old Baron was so elevated with this happy union of his descendants, that he cried out—Now I am ready to die! I have lived long enough! this is the band of love that unites all my children to me, and to each other! He did not long survive this happy event; he died full of years and honours, and his name was never mentioned but with the deepest marks of gratitude, love and veneration. Sweet is the remembrance of the virtuous, and happy are the descendants of such a father! they will think on him and emulate his virtues; they will remember him, and be ashamed to degenerate from their ancestor.

Many years after Sir Philip Harclay settled at the Castle, he received tidings from his friend Zadisky, by one of the two servants who attended him to the Holy Land. From him he learned that his friend had discovered, by private advices, that he had a son living in Palestine, which was the chief motive of his leaving England; that he met with various adventures in pursuit of him; that at length he found him, converted him to the christian religion, and then persuaded him to retire from the world into a monastery by the side of mount Libanus,* where he intended to end his days.

That Walter, commonly called Lord Lovel, had entered into the service of the Greek emperor, John Paleologus,* not bearing to undergo a life of solitude and retirement; that he made up a story of his being compelled to leave his native country by his relations, for having accidentally killed one of them, and that he was treated with great cruelty and injustice; that he had accepted a post in the emperor's army, and was soon after married to the daughter of one of the chief officers of it.

Zadisky foresaw, and lamented the downfall of that empire,* and withdrew from the storm he saw approaching. Finally, he bade the messenger tell Sir Philip Harclay and his adopted son, that he should not cease to pray for them, and desired their prayers in return.

Sir Philip desired Lord Lovel to entertain this messenger in his service. That good knight lived to extreme old age in honour and happiness, and died in the arms of his beloved Edmund; who also performed the last duties to his faithful Joseph.

Father Oswald lived many years in the family as chaplain; he retired from thence at length, and died in his own monastery.

Edmund Lord Lovel lived to old age, in peace, honour and happiness; and died in the arms of his children.

Sir Philip Harclay caused the papers relating to his son's history to be collected together; the first part of it was written under his own eye in Yorkshire, the subsequent parts by Father Oswald

136   *The Old English Baron*

at the Castle of Lovel. All these, when together, furnish a striking
lesson to posterity, of the over-ruling hand of Providence, and the
certainty of RETRIBUTION.

FINIS

APPENDIX 1

FROM *THE CHAMPION OF VIRTUE* (1777)

ADDRESS TO THE READER

READER, before you enter upon the history before you, permit the Author to hold a short conference with you, upon certain points that will elucidate the design, and perhaps induce you to form a *favourable*, as well as a right judgment of the work.

Pray did you ever read a book called, The Castle of Otranto? if you have, you will willingly enter with me into a review of it.—but perhaps you have not read it? however you have heard that it is an attempt to blend together, the most attractive and interesting circumstances of the ancient romance and modern Novel; but possibly you may not know so much, *still* you have read *some* ancient Romance, or *some* modern Novel, it will be strange if you have not in this age!

But suppose you should dislike or despise them both? 'tis no matter! I shall catch you some way or other.

You delight in the fables of the ancients, the old poets, or story-tellers.

Or, you are pleased with the wonderful adventures of modern travellers, such as Gaudentio di Lucca, or Robinson Crusoe.*

Or, if you are unacquainted with any of the books already mentioned, I would venture a good wager that you have read the Pilgrim's Progress.*

You smile! but I mean nothing ludicrous, the Pilgrim's Progress is a work of genius, and as such I respect it.—is it possible that a book merely fanatical, should have run through fifty-four editions? you may safely conclude it has merit of a higher kind, that enables it to blunt the shafts of ridicule, and to stand its ground, notwithstanding the variations of times and tastes, and the refinements of literature and language.

But what (say you) is all this to the purpose? patience a moment, and I will come directly to the point.—if you have read any *fictitious* or *fabulous* story, it will answer my intention, which is to assert, that all readers, of all times and countries have delighted in stories of these kinds; and that those who affect to despise them under one form, will receive and embrace them in another.

History represents human nature as it is.—alas! too often a melancholy retrospect—romance displays only the amiable side of the picture; it shows the pleasing features, and throws a veil over the blemishes: mankind are naturally pleased with what gratifies their vanity, and vanity like all other passions of the human heart, may be rendered subservient to good and useful purposes.

I confess that it may be abused, and become an instrument to corrupt the manners and morals of mankind; so may poetry, so may plays, so may every kind of composition; but that will prove nothing more than the old saying lately revived—'that every earthly thing has two handles.'

The business of romance is first to excite the attention, and secondly to direct it to some useful, or at least innocent end. Happy the writer who attains both these points, like Richardson! and not unfortunate, or undeserving of praise, he who gains only the latter, and furnishes out of it an entertainment for the reader!

Having, in some degree, opened my design, I beg leave to conduct my reader back again, till he comes within view of the castle of Otranto; a work which has already been observed, is an attempt to unite the various merits and graces of the ancient romance and modern Novel.—to attain this end, there is required a sufficient degree of the marvellous to excite the attention.—enough of the manners of real life, to give an air of probability to the work;—and enough of the pathetic to engage the heart in its behalf.

The book before us is excellent in the two last points, but has a redundancy in the first; the opening excites the attention very strongly; the conduct of the story is artful and judicious; the characters are admirably drawn and supported; the diction polished and elegant; yet with all these brilliant advantages, it palls upon the mind, though it does not upon the ear, and the reason is obvious; the machinery is so violent, that it destroys the effect it is intended to excite. Had the story been kept within the utmost *verge* of probability, the effect had been preserved, without losing the least circumstance that excites or detains the attention.

For instance, we can conceive and allow of the appearance of a ghost, we can even dispense with an enchanted sword and helmet, but then they must keep within certain limits of credibility, a sword so large as to require an hundred men to lift it, a helmet that by its own weight forces a passage through a court-yard into an arched vault, big enough for a man to go through; a picture that walks out of its frame; a skeleton ghost in a hermit's cowl: when your expectation is wound up to the highest pitch, these circumstances take it down with a witness, destroy the work of imagination, and instead of attention, excite laughter. I was both surprised and vexed to find the enchantment dissolved, that I wished might continue to the end of the book, and several others of its readers have confessed the same disappointment to me; the beauties are so numerous, that we cannot bear the defects, but want it to be perfect in all respects.

In the course of my observations upon this singular book, it seemed to me that it was possible to compose a work upon the same plan, wherein these defects might be avoided, and the *keeping* as in *painting* might be preserved.

But then, said I, it might happen to the writer as it has to the imitators of Shakespeare, the *unities* may be preserved, but the *spirit* may evaporate; in short it will be safest to let it alone.

During these reflections, it occurred to my remembrance, that a certain friend of mine was in possession of a manuscript in the old English language, containing a story that answered in almost every point to the plan above-mentioned; and if it were modernised, might afford entertainment to those who delight in stories of this kind.

Accordingly (with my friend's permission) I transcribed, or rather translated a few sheets of it.—I read it to a circle of friends of approved judgment, they gave me the warmest encouragement to proceed, and even made me promise to finish it.

Here it is, therefore, at your service; if you are pleased, I am satisfied; I will venture to assure you that it shall not leave you worse than it finds you in any respect. If you despise the work it will go to sleep quietly with many of its contemporaries, and the *ghost of it* will not disturb your repose.

> I am, with profound Respect,
> Reader, your most obedient Servant,
> The EDITOR.*

APPENDIX 2

DEDICATION TO MRS. BRIDGEN*

MADAM,

This new Edition of the *English Baron* begs permission to acknowledge your patronage and protection, of which it has long since felt the advantages.

You cast an eye of favour upon his first appearance, under all the disadvantages of an incorrect and very faulty impression. You took him out of this degrading dress, and encouraged him to assume a graceful and ornamental habit.

You did still more for him. You took upon yourself the trouble to revise and correct the errors of the first impression; and, in short, you gave him all the graces necessary to solicit and obtain the notice and approbation of the public.

The Author cannot fully enjoy her success without acknowledging from whence she in great measure derives it.

You, Madam, as becomes the daughter of Richardson, are more solicitous to deserve the acknowledgements of a grateful heart, than to receive them. You have no reason to suspect me of flattery, but of vanity you may, in wishing to mention your name thus publicly as the patroness and friend of,

Madam,

Your most obliged humble Servant
CLARA REEVE

Sept. 1, 1780.

EXPLANATORY NOTES

2 *the Castle of Otranto*: the title of Horace Walpole's ground-breaking Gothic romance, first published pseudonymously in 1764.

the appellation of a Gothic Story: Walpole had used this label on the title page of *The Castle of Otranto*'s second edition, published in 1765.

only Epics in prose: Reeve examined the opposition between epic and romance at much greater length in her ambitious work of literary history, *The Progress of Romance* (1785). She sought to rehabilitate and revalue romance, in part by emphasizing its past kinship with epic.

the amiable side of the picture: Reeve's distinction between History and Romance echoes the contrast drawn by Sir Philip Sidney between the 'brazen' world of nature and the 'golden' world of poetry. See Sidney, *An Apology for Poetry*, ed. Geoffrey Shepherd (Manchester: Manchester University Press, 1973), 24.

'every earthly thing has two handles': a maxim of the Stoic philosopher Epictetus (*c.* AD 60–140). Reeve would perhaps have known Elizabeth Carter's 1758 translation of *All the Works of Epictetus*, although she would also have been able to read the original, having already translated the Latin of Barclay's *Argenis* in 1772.

3 *Richardson*: Samuel Richardson (1689–1761), author of the novels *Pamela*, *Clarissa*, and *Sir Charles Grandison*; also father of Martha Bridgen, who advised—and perhaps directed—Reeve during the revision of *The Champion of Virtue* into *The Old English Baron* (see Note on the Text).

A sword so large … a hermit's cowl: features of, or incidents from, Walpole's *The Castle of Otranto*.

4 *the keeping, as in painting*: harmony of composition.

the unities: principles of dramatic composition derived from Aristotle's *Poetics*.

the former Edition being very incorrect: see Note on the Text.

as that character is thought to be the principal one in the story: note, however, Scott's observation about the marginality of the title character: 'if Fitz-owen be considered as the Old English Baron, we do not see wherefore a character, passive in himself from beginning to end, and only acted upon by others, should be selected to give a theme to the story' ('Prefatory Memoir to Clara Reeve', *The Novels of Sterne, Goldsmith, Dr Johnson, Mackenzie, Horace Walpole and Clara Reeve. To which are prefixed, Memoirs of the Lives of the Authors*, Novelist's Library (Edinburgh, 1823), vol. v, p. lxx. For Anna Laetitia Barbauld, the 'old baron' of the title is Sir

Philip Harclay—'a fine character' (*The British Novelists* (London, 1810), vol. xxii, p. ii).

5 *the minority of . . . Protector of England*: the son of Henry V, Henry VI acceded to the throne as an infant in 1422, and formally came of age in 1437; John, Duke of Bedford, was brother of Henry V, and from 1422 his successor as English military commander in France; Humphrey, Duke of Gloucester, uncle of Henry VI, was Protector during his nephew's minority.

the glorious King Henry the Fifth: King of England between 1413 and 1422, best known for his victory over the French at the Battle of Agincourt in 1415.

the Greek Emperor: John Paleologus, Emperor of Byzantium between 1421 and 1448.

the Saracens: generic term for the nomadic peoples of the Arabian desert, popularized during and after the Crusades; used by Reeve to refer to the Ottoman Turks who were encroaching upon the territories of the declining Byzantine Empire.

7 *Welch Rebels*: Wales was conquered in the late thirteenth century during the reign of Edward I, but continued to present problems of order and security for later English monarchs. Baron Fitz-Owen has a castle in Wales, later inherited by Edmund's third son William (p. 134). The name Fitz-Owen—'son of Owen'—might be seen to allude to the figure of Owen Glendower (d.1415), the most famous of the Welsh leaders during this period, but Reeve doesn't pursue this connection.

10 *an angel of gold*: a gold coin depicting the archangel Michael standing upon, and piercing the dragon—an anachronistic detail, since the angel was not coined in England until 1465, during the reign of Edward IV.

15 *a strong resemblance he bears to a certain dear friend I once had*: cf. Theodore's physical likeness to portraits of Alfonso the Good in Walpole's *Otranto*; Edmund is later struck by the portraits of the late Lord and Lady Lovel in the haunted apartment (pp. 47–8).

19 *as by the manuscript*: Reeve omits to delete this detail, even though *The Old English Baron* no longer presents itself as the translation of an ancient manuscript (see Note on the Text).

prognosticks: predictions or prophecies.

20 *France . . . the art of war*: large areas of France were occupied by the English in the early fifteenth century. By the Treaty of Troyes in 1420, Henry V was made Regent of France, and heir to the Valois throne ahead of the Dauphin (see below). Henry V never became king of France, dying only two years later, but Henry VI, his son, inherited the claim to dual monarchy.

22 *cabal*: a secret or private grouping of intriguers—first recorded uses occur in the mid seventeenth century.

the great Duke of Bedford: the Duke of Bedford died in 1435; by 1453, only Calais remained of Henry V's French possessions.

Richard Plantagenet, Duke of York: cousin of Henry VI, later appointed protector of the realm during the king's mental and physical collapse in 1454–5 and 1455–6.

Charles the Dauphin: 'Dauphin' was the title of the direct heir to the French throne; Charles VII was crowned king in 1429. As Reeve acknowledges, the period of Charles's rule saw the resurgence of opposition to the English presence in France.

28 *Henry the Fourth*: King of England between 1399 and 1413; the deaths of Lord and Lady Lovel are said to have occurred during his reign.

29 *St. Austin's church*: a contraction of St Augustine (d. 604), founder of the Christian Church in England.

31 *as Jonathan did to David*: 'And Saul spake to Jonathan his son, and to all his servants, that they should kill David. But Jonathan Saul's son delighted much in David: and Jonathan told David, saying, Saul my father seeketh to kill thee: now therefore, I pray thee, take heed to thyself until the morning, and abide in a secret place, and hide thyself' (1 Samuel 19: 1–2). William Fitz-Owen, however, warns Edmund about the conduct of his brothers rather than his father.

37 *if the spirit appears visibly, I will speak to it*: cf. Hamlet's address to the ghost of his father: 'Go on, I'll follow thee!' (I. iv. 63). Reeve followed Walpole's example by resorting to the ghost scenes from *Hamlet* as a model for the representation of the supernatural.

40 *Manage*: an enclosed space for the training of saddle-horses and for the practice of horsemanship; a riding school (*OED*).

41 *Caradoc*: Caradoc, or Caractacus (d. *c.* AD 54), was a leader of the Britons in their resistance to Roman invasion; he was finally defeated at Colchester (where Reeve lived for much of her adult life).

saucy: 'insolent towards superiors' or 'scornful, disdainful' (*OED*); perhaps the latter sense is most appropriate here.

46 *paternoster*: the Lord's Prayer, especially in the Latin version—a usage consistent with Reeve's relatively neutral representation of Catholicism (compare Margery Twyford's exclamations of 'Blessed Virgin!' and 'Holy Virgin!' on pp. 49, 53).

49 *Goody*: a term of civility applied to a woman, usually a married woman, of humble status.

68 *a man in compleat armour . . . with one hand extended*: cf. the marching spectre of Manfred's grandfather, descending from his portrait, in Walpole's *Otranto*. Reeve also follows Walpole's account of the domestics Diego and Jaquez, in their encounter with the fragments of armour from Alfonso's statue.

72 *Saint Winifred*: (d. *c.*650), patron saint of north Wales. According to

legend, she was sought in marriage by Prince Caradog of Hawarden, but refused his advances. Different versions of the story state that she was either wounded or killed by Caradog, and then healed or miraculously restored to life by her uncle, St Beuno. A spring marked the spot— the present Holywell, Clwyd—where St Winifred later established a monastery.

81 *the Scottish marches*: the contested border area that separated England from Scotland.

87 *e fructu arbor cognoscitur*: the tree is known by its fruit.

91 *shut up these one and twenty years*: given that the Lord Lovel who appears in Sir Philip Harclay's dream has been dead 'these fifteen years' (p. 11), this detail suggests that the action of the book takes place over the course of six years.

110 *ingraft*: implant or incorporate (*OED*).

113 *The nominal Baron*: the usurping Sir Walter Lovel.

128 *the certaintie of Retribution*: Reeve's transcription of 'medieval' English was perhaps influenced by the Rowley poems of Thomas Chatterton (1752–70), presented as the work of a fifteenth-century monk.

135 *mount Libanus*: in present-day Lebanon.

John Paleologus: Byzantine Emperor between 1421 and 1448.

the downfall of that empire: the Byzantine Empire fell with the capture of Constantinople by the Turks in 1453.

137 *Gaudentio di Lucca, or Robinson Crusoe*: Simon Berington, *The Memoirs of Signior Gaudentio di Lucca: Taken from his Confession and Examination before the Fathers of the Inquisition at Bologna in Italy; Making a Discovery of an Unknown Country in the Midst of the Vast Deserts of Africa* (1737), a popular imaginary travel narrative; Daniel Defoe, *The Life and Strange and Surprising Adventures of Robinson Crusoe* (1719), the famous narrative of the fictitious desert island castaway.

the Pilgrim's Progress: *The Pilgrim's Progress, from this World to that which is to come* (Part I 1678, Part II 1684), John Bunyan's popular and influential religious allegory.

139 *The EDITOR*: following the practice of Walpole in the first edition of *The Castle of Otranto*, Reeve initially presented herself as the editor of a recovered manuscript, rather than as the author of a novel or romance; like Walpole she abandoned this device in the second edition of her work.

140 *MRS. BRIDGEN*: Martha Bridgen, daughter of Samuel Richardson (for Bridgen's involvement in the revision of *The Champion of Virtue*, see Note on the Text).